Jonathan knew he must have Sarah... but on her terms.

"I apologize if you were sleeping, but I couldn't let the night pass without telling you how sorry I am for what I tried to do."

Though he looked sincere, Sarah had no pity for him. "I've no father, I can't read, and I've been a servant all my life," she said evenly. "Because of that, people have looked at me as lowborn since I was a little girl."

"But I don't—"

"Yes, sir, you do," she interrupted. "You think you can buy me a pretty dress and say pleasant things to me and then have your way with me because I'm too ignorant to know any better."

His face clouding, Jonathan opened his mouth as if to speak, but Sarah jumped in once more. "I don't have much, but the one thing I know is that I'm a lady. A lady, like my mother was. And you won't take that away from me, sir!"

KATE BLACKWELL is a former kindergarten teacher who now stays home to pursue her lifelong dream of writing novels. This novel, her first, is a fulfillment of that dream.

Shores
of Promise

Kate Blackwell

Heartsong Presents

ISBN 1-55748-362-0

SHORES OF PROMISE

one
1840

Please still be there, thought Sarah Brown as she rounded the corner of the house from the back. Her pulse quickened—the carriage was just about to pull away from the front gate! Gathering her skirts with her right hand and waving her left, she hastened her steps.

"Ma'am!" she called out, no longer caring if the occupants of the house heard her. The driver flicked his short whip over the horse's back. With a creak of wood and iron, the carriage started to roll, leaving Sarah too far away to catch up. Filling her lungs with deep gulps of air, she looked back at the house. Mrs. Gerty's face was at an upstairs window.

I'm done for now, Sarah thought, unable to tear her eyes away from the woman's frowning face. The sound of horses' hooves pierced through the fog of despair that engulfed her. The carriage was returning!

Spurred on by renewed hope, Sarah ran toward the carriage. Just as she could make out the puzzled look on Mrs. Carlton's face, disaster struck. The toe of Sarah's worn leather slipper caught in the hem of her dress. Down she went with a violent thud!

"My dear, are you all right?" Sarah was too mortified to move. Two hands gently pulled at her shoulder and arm, and she allowed the driver to help her to her feet. Her teeth were gritty with dirt, and there was blood on her fingers when she pulled them away from the burning place on her cheek.

Sarah knew she was a sight, but the woman in the carriage looked at her with such concern that it gave her courage to speak. "Ma'am," she began, taking a deep breath and walking over to the buggy. "You said you'd be needing a maid?"

Mrs. Carlton pulled out a lace-bordered handkerchief from a lavender beaded purse. She leaned forward and held it out to Sarah, pushing it into her hand when the girl appeared reluctant to touch the fine piece of linen.

"Now, what's that you're asking?" she said as Sarah held the handkerchief to her cheek.

"A maid. I heard you say that you'd like to have an English serving maid. I'm a hard worker. Do you think you could take me on?"

Mrs. Carlton turned toward the house, and Sarah looked back over her shoulder. Mrs. Gerty had moved from the window to the front doorway. She was too far away to hear their conversation, but the glare on her red-splotched face told Sarah that the woman had an idea of what was taking place. Sarah turned back to Mrs. Carlton.

"You wouldn't even have to pay me," she said quickly. "I'll work for board, and I don't eat much."

The older woman laughed, but her voice was full of compassion. "You work for Mrs. Gerty, dear. I can't go stealing you away. Besides, I was just making conversation when I spoke of wanting a maid. We really have enough servants."

Sarah opened her mouth to speak, then closed it again. "Yes'm," she said as she took a step back from the buggy, lowering her head. "I'm sorry to have disturbed you."

Mrs. Gerty's eyes burned into her back, and Sarah knew she'd have to face those eyes as she walked back to the house. The thought filled her with such dread that her courage came back. She took a step forward.

"Please?" She looked directly into Mrs. Carlton's eyes, putting all her longing into her gaze.

Mrs. Carlton held a crochet-gloved hand up to her lined cheek. The girl that stood in front of her was a bit pale—probably from working long hours indoors—but there was a captivating freshness about her. The slightly upturned nose and wide brown eyes contrasted interestingly with the determined straight line of her lips.

"Well, I suppose it would be nice to have you serving my guests. You are quite lovely." Sarah's cry of joy was cut short when Mrs. Carlton held up a hand. "I must discuss this with my husband." Catching the slight drop of the girl's shoulders, Mrs. Carlton reached out and patted her on the arm. "Don't worry. He does everything I ask him, but it makes him feel good to have me ask. You understand?"

Sarah's smile returned. "Yes ma'am. Oh, thank you ma'am!"

Mrs. Carlton smiled back. "Now, we're leaving Bristol to go back to the States in two days. Meet us at the dock, and I'm sure we'll have your passage ready. Should I send a carriage for you?"

"Could I come with you now?" asked Sarah, fearful that Mrs. Carlton would change her mind if pressed too hard, but more afraid of facing Mrs. Gerty.

Mrs. Carlton studied Sarah's face. "How old are you, dear?"

"Sixteen, ma'am."

"Are things so bad here?"

"Yes'm," Sarah cried, embarrassed by the tears that gathered in her eyes. "I can't go back, not now!"

"Well, climb on in then!" Mrs. Carlton said. The driver, stately in his blue velvet waistcoat adorned with a row of gold buttons, had been patiently standing to the side. Upon hearing Mrs. Carlton's invitation, he helped Sarah into the seat next to her. When Sarah was settled in the carriage, Mrs. Carlton turned to her. "Don't you need to get some belongings from the house?"

Sarah shuddered. "There's naught that I care about. My other dress is quite worn. I just wear it when I wash this one."

Reaching deep into the pocket of her apron, Sarah drew out a bundle of coins bound up in a shabby piece of muslin, the savings she'd grabbed from her attic room when she realized Mrs. Carlton was leaving. "I can buy another dress—maybe two—so's you won't be ashamed of me."

Mrs. Carlton let out a hearty chuckle. "My dear, no one will ever be ashamed of you!" Instructing the driver to turn the carriage around, she turned her face toward Mrs. Gerty, who stood glowering.

"I didn't like that woman, anyway," she said to Sarah with a grin.

Sarah couldn't help but look back, not at Mrs. Gerty, but at the house. Most people thought Gothic-style Connelsworth Park—with its delicate bay windows and crocketed pinnacles—was majestic as any cathedral. Three years of her life had been spent there, and to Sarah no prison could have been uglier.

two
1834

Sarah's earliest memories were of her mother's skirts swishing as she cooked in the lofty kitchen at Hadenwilde Manor. A wooden spoon and tin soup ladle served as Sarah's toys, and she quickly learned that they'd be taken away if she banged them on the stone-flagged floor.

The kitchen was toasty during damp winter months, a wonderful escape from the unheated servants' quarters. The summer months, however, were plain misery. Steam rose from the copper cooking pots, bathing Ruth, Sarah's mother, in sweat. Alice, the kitchen maid, was equally wretched.

Still, the heat was more tolerable near the floor where Sarah played and napped. Comfort and companionship could be had by toddling over to her mother and grabbing a handful of muslin skirt to hold next to her cheek. When Ruth needed to move to another part of the kitchen, she'd gently tug on her skirt to release it from the grip of those baby fingers.

As Sarah grew, she was given more chores to perform in the great kitchen. She was a willing helper and quick learner. By the age of five, she created almost transparent peelings from potatoes and beets, and by age six she could knead and fold a mountain of bread dough. Staying busy made the day pass more quickly, and when her legs ached from long hours of standing, she looked ahead to when the last meal would be served and the kitchen cleaned and polished.

"Little Sarah, let's have a walk!" her mother would say, wiping her hands on her apron. Then the two would slip out of the house and sit on a bench in the garden—if none of the owner's family or guests were there—before retiring to the tiny room they shared with Alice.

It didn't matter to the little girl that darkness prevented them from seeing the full glory of the delphiniums and roses. She could lean back and see stars peeking through holes in the sky. Often Sarah would rest her head on her mother's lap, her face pointed toward heaven, as she listened to her mother's lovely singing.

> *"See the stars, like little candles*
> *In the deep, dark sky*
> *And the maid who comes to light them*
> *She'll sleep by and by."*

Sarah liked to wonder, with a trace of envy, about the girl who had such an important responsibility. Was she as pretty as her mother, who had faint dimples at the corners of her mouth and eyes as dark as mulberries? The delivery men who brought meat or butter and eggs to the kitchen always gave her mother special attention. While Alice was ready to lean against the door frame and chat with them, Sarah's mother treated them with cool politeness.

As the evening passed, the little girl's thoughts would muddle into dreams about butter and mulberries and floating through night breezes from star to star with a fiery torch. The next thing she'd be aware of was waking up in the morning between Mother and Alice on the goose-feather mattress.

One night, ten-year-old Sarah wasn't interested in the stars. A thought had troubled her since the night before. She sat on the bench in silence, needing consolation for her pain but afraid of what dreadful things she might learn.

Though not permitted in the rooms of the house where the

Norton family lived, Sarah had been called upon several times to help serve a meal, especially when the family entertained guests.

"Don't be a calling any attention to yourself, little Sarah," her mother had warned, so Sarah had tried to move silently. The previous evening had been particularly busy. All sixteen places had been filled by the guests and their hosts, Henry and Anne Norton. The Nortons' five children had been sent to bed hours earlier, and the adults were being served a late dinner after their return from a performance of "Venice Preserv'd" at the Grafton Street Theatre.

"I ain't never seen the likes of so much food!" Celly, the new serving girl, had said as she'd loaded her tray in the kitchen. Ignoring a sharp look from Ruth, she'd fingered a sliver of baked whitefish from one of the dishes and popped it into her mouth.

"Jobs is scarce around here, lessin' you want to lose your eyesight at the weaver's mill," Ruth had warned. "I wouldn't go upsetting the mistress if I was you."

Celly's cheeks had nearly matched her flaming red hair as, lips drawn into a pout, she'd haughtily tossed her head and joined Sarah and the other serving girl bringing trays back and forth from the kitchen. The meal had started out with soup, fish, meat and game, sauces, vegetables, and a sweet pudding.

After the first course, the girls had reset the table, working around the diners. The second course had included several main dishes of meat and fish and a variety of puddings, creams, and tarts.

For the dessert course, the white damask tablecloth had been removed and the table reset with fruits, pastries, jellies, and other sweetmeats, all enticingly displayed in crystal or silver dishes. Once the desserts were served, Sarah only had to stand near the sideboard table and watch to see if her services were needed. Though she didn't understand the gossip that was tittered over, it was fascinating to a little girl who spent most of her time in the kitchen.

That evening, Sarah had been so absorbed in the lively chatter that it had taken her a few seconds to realize a young lady was motioning to her. With a start, Sarah had gone to her side.

"I've dropped my napkin. Please bring me another." The lady had been wearing a white crepe dress trimmed with pink satin ribbon, the bodice and sleeves spotted with white beads. Her flaxen hair had been bound up with several pearl combs, and Sarah was sure she'd never seen anyone so elegant. The lady had been seated next to Thorton Hepplewhite, Mrs. Norton's younger brother. Mr. Hepplewhite was often a guest at the table, but he had never taken notice of the servants. Sarah had been surprised when, as she had retrieved a clean linen napkin, she'd overheard him speak her name to his companion.

"Her name is Sarah," he had said, obviously in answer to the lady's inquiry.

The lady had looked over her shoulder at Sarah and smiled, then had turned back to Thorton. "She's a beautiful child! Where did she come from?" she'd asked, loudly enough for the other diners to hear.

Sarah had wanted to run to the lady's side and throw herself at her feet. Beautiful! No one other than her mother had ever called her that. Turning her head, Sarah had sought her reflection in the silver tea pitcher sitting on the sideboard. Her distorted reflection had revealed thickly lashed brown eyes and fine cheekbones. Curly tendrils of chestnut hair framed her oval face. Turning back to the table, Sarah had wondered what Mr. Hepplewhite was whispering to the lady that made her cover her mouth and laugh softly.

"What did he say, deary?" Across the table from the couple, a dark-haired woman in a green-sprigged muslin dress was leaning forward. "Where did she come from?" The woman made no effort to lower her voice.

That was when it had happened. The fine lady, with another glance over her shoulder at Sarah, had leaned forward. Her voice had been low, but just as she whispered her response, other conversation ceased. Sarah, who had pretended not to listen, heard an expression that had turned her blood to ice.

Her heart hammering in her throat, Sarah had stood with her back to the wall, feigning ignorance. Some of the more ill-mannered guests had stared at her before turning to whisper to a neighbor. Others had given Sarah quick glances, pretending interest in the silver tea service at her side or the portraits on the wall above her. The lady sitting next to Mr. Hepplewhite had not looked at her again.

Sarah shuddered as the memory of that evening came back to her. All day, she'd managed to keep busy and let work occupy her thoughts. But sitting in the cool night air, nothing could keep her from reliving the experience.

"Are you cold, Sarah?" Her mother put an arm around Sarah's shoulder and pulled her closer. Sarah snuggled against her mother's side, closing her eyes tightly and trying to feel the way she had until last night—that Mother was her whole world.

She marveled that she had never wondered why she didn't have a father. Oh, she'd known about fathers. She saw how kind Mr. Norton was to his children, but she'd assumed that wealthy children had fathers just like they had fine clothes and toys and ponies. Poor children had none of those things.

When she'd heard Jake the gardener use the wretched word that the elegant lady had whispered, she'd had to ask Alice what it meant. When she'd been told, she'd shrugged her shoulders—it had nothing to do with her.

Now she knew. Her very existence was a profanity! A great sob tore her throat.

"Sarah?" Her mother's voice was filled with alarm as she turned Sarah to face her. "Whatever is wrong?"

Clinging to her mother's arms, Sarah wept on. Finally, her chest heaving and her throat raw, she sat up and wiped her nose on the hem of her apron. "Mother," she managed to whisper. "Why don't I have a father?"

Shoulders sagging, Ruth let out a long sigh, her lips trembling. Sarah wished that she hadn't spoken. She looked down at her mother's work-roughened hands—hands that caressed her when she needed comfort. Filled with shame for hurting the woman who'd only been good to her, Sarah reached up and put her hand on her mother's cheek.

Just then, Ruth spoke. "I used to have Sundays off—did you know that?" She was looking straight ahead. "And I was paid twice what I'm paid now."

She was quiet for so long that Sarah wondered if her mother had fallen asleep. Then she spoke again. "I had a friend who worked here until she got married to a shipyard worker. Her name was Kate. We was real good friends, and about once a month Ben, the livery man, would take the vegetable wagon in to Bristol and visit his family. He'd drop me off near Kate's, and we'd have a lovely time, Kate and me and her husband, John." She smiled faintly, reliving happier days.

"Sometimes John's brother, Thomas, would come by. He seemed to like me. I was only eighteen and so shy, but I liked him, too. He was quiet, like me."

Taking a deep breath, she continued. "The little cottage Kate lived in was down a dirt lane that was too narrow for the wagon. There must have been hundreds of cottages thrown together there. When Ben let me out of the wagon, I had to walk past alleys and buildings and cottages to get to Kate's. We always went there in the daytime and there was plenty of people around, so I never thought I was in danger.

"I never heard the man when he came up behind me from the alley!" Sarah's mother said, her voice quivering. "After. . .I didn't even go to Kate's. I was so ashamed!" Her lips tightened. "I was raised to be a good girl, Sarah, but some men are evil.

"When I discovered that I was in a family way, I didn't know what to do. My grandmother had died when I was fourteen, and I never had no other family. Lonely and scared I was."

For a while mother and daughter sat holding hands. Sarah was stunned. She knew about babies and how they were made, but she'd never heard of anything so brutal.

"When Mrs. Norton found out, she told me she would have to dismiss me because I would shame her family and be a bad example to her daughters and the other servants. She said that none of the ladies she knew would want to hire me, either. I didn't have no other place to go, so I got down on my knees and begged her not to make me leave. After she talked to Master Norton about it, she offered to let me stay if I'd work for half-wages and no Sundays off."

Finding her voice, Sarah asked, "What about Thomas?"

"I never went back to Kate's, and when they sent me messages, I didn't get anyone to read them to me. I threw them away."

"You never saw him again?"

"Thomas came to see me a few months later. Alice was new, and she let him in before I could see who it was." Ruth's voice turned flat. "I stood there, big with child, and he didn't say a word. He stared at me. Then he turned and left."

Sarah's heart filled with rage at the man who'd hurt her mother and at the Nortons for treating her so badly. Her anger turned inward when she realized that she herself was the cause of her mother's troubles. Fresh tears came to her eyes. "Are you sorry you have me?"

Ruth hugged her daughter tightly, almost squeezing her breath away. "Never! After you was born, I loved you from the start."

Sarah wasn't sure how long they sat together that evening, but her first thought the next morning was that she would never let anyone hurt her mother like that again.

three
1837

"Mercy!" exclaimed Celly, pushing her chair back from the scarred kitchen table. "It's terrible hot in here!" She stretched out her legs and fanned them with the hem of her skirt.

Thirteen-year-old Sarah watched as her mother and Alice exchanged raised eyebrows. Celly had managed to sit by George, and the pock-marked stable boy was gawking at her white shins. Embarrassed for the older girl, Sarah cleared her throat, hoping Celly would notice the attention she was drawing.

Celly looked up. With a self-conscious giggle, she smoothed her skirt back over her legs and gave George a smile. Red-faced, George snapped his mouth shut and turned his eyes back to his plate of food.

"I don't see why you had to bake bread today, with the rain pourin' down like that," Celly whined, turning to Ruth. "We can't even take our dinner outside."

Ruth stopped cutting wedges from a fist-sized ball of hoop cheese. "The missus and family are comin' home from holiday tomorrow. I'll be needing some bread. But it's only light misting outside. You can carry your plate under the arbor if you're wantin' some air."

Fluttering her eyelashes, Celly smiled at George again. "I've a mind to do that. Would anyone be wantin' to join me?"

"That's a right fine idea!" From across the table, Jake, the gardener, flashed Celly a yellow-toothed grin as he picked up his plate and fork. "I'm sufferin' greatly in this kitchen!"

Glancing at George hunched over his plate spooning mutton stew into his mouth, Celly pulled her chair back up to the

17

table. "It ain't so bad in here."

Sarah thought about the arbor. It would be great fun to sit on the stone bench and listen to the raindrops pelt the grapevine leaves that carpeted the trellis. She could almost smell the earthy aroma of wet leaves and damp air.

"Why don't you go, Celly?" she said, hoping that if the girl changed her mind and went with Jake, they would invite her along. "It's so pretty there."

"I said it ain't so bad in here." Celly gave Sarah a withering look.

"I'll go with ye, Sarah," said George, sitting up in his chair and wiping his mouth with the back of his sleeve. "I like the rain."

Sarah was fond of George. She was about to agree when she caught Celly's expression. The older girl was staring at her with such an outpouring of anger that Sarah was shaken. *Why, Celly hates me!* she thought. Confused, she tried to think of what she'd done to deserve such malice. Was it because George offered to go outside with her?

Wishing she hadn't said anything, Sarah was relieved when her mother spoke. "I'll be needin' Sarah to help me in a few minutes. She'd best stay here."

Sarah stole another look at Celly, expecting everything would be back to normal. Celly's expression hadn't changed.

The next day was unusually busy as the servants hurried to get the house ready for the family.

"Master Henry and the family are here!" called out Fenton, the butler. The other house servants scurried to the great hall and, with much whispering and nervous excitement, took their places according to their importance in the household.

Fenton stood first in line. Albert, the footman and only other male house servant, had accompanied the Nortons on holiday, so the female servants took their places after the butler. At any other estate, the cook would have been second only to the housekeeper among the female staff, but at Hadenwilde Manor that had changed more than a decade earlier. Ruth stood at the end of the line behind Ester, the scullery maid. Sarah, who was allowed to work in the kitchen but received no salary, stood last, next to her mother.

The whispering ceased when the massive carved oak doors swung open. Albert was the first to enter, quickly standing to the side to hold one of the doors, while Fenton held the other one.

"Good evening, Master Henry!" chorused the line of servants as Henry Norton entered, carrying three-year-old Jenny Norton in his arms. His gray frock coat and nankeen trousers were uncustomarily wrinkled from the long carriage ride, and the familiar musty-sweet odor of pipe tobacco trailed behind him.

Henry Norton nodded, handing the sleeping child over to Frances, a stocky housemaid. "Put her to bed. Mind you take her shoes off," he ordered. Turning to his wife, who was coming through the doorway, he motioned toward his study. "I'll be looking over the books. Have supper sent to me when it's ready."

Anne Norton frowned at her husband's back, ignoring the greetings of the servants. "So, this is why you were so anxious to get back home. You think a fortnight away from business has ruined us?"

Mr. Norton froze, opened his mouth as if to speak, and then continued on to his study without looking back.

Sarah felt sorry for Mrs. Norton. The slender woman's pinched face had fallen, and the corners of her eyes were glistening with tears. Remembering the way her mother was being treated by this family brought her sympathy to a sharp end, but she was still uncomfortable in the sight of such distress.

"Emily, I've a headache," Mrs. Norton said to the governess, who had Frank, Elizabeth, and Celeste in tow. "See that the children are bathed before supper." The mistress of the house took to the stairs with her personal maid, Penelope, following.

As soon as the Norton family had left the room, the servants scattered, some heading out to the carriage to bring in chests of clothing, some to the dining room to set the table for supper. The kitchen workers, Ruth, Alice, and Sarah, returned to their preparations for the meal.

"Sarah, give me a hand." Ruth was folding towels to handle the iron door of the brick oven. A blast of scorched air stirred the wisps of dark hair around her forehead as she bent down to remove a sizzling roaster.

Sarah fetched a pewter platter from the cupboard and brought it to the kitchen table, where her mother was setting the hot pan. Using three-pronged meat forks, she helped lift a crisp goose onto the platter.

"There ain't much prettier than a roast goose!" said Ruth, spooning drippings from the pan over the bird. "I believe this is the—"

Her words were interrupted by a commotion at the kitchen door. Sarah and her mother looked up in surprise to see Anne Norton burst through the door, followed by Mrs. Owen, the housekeeper.

"I would like to see all of you in the front!" Mrs. Norton ordered, her eyes red and swollen. A lady of quality never set foot in her own kitchen, so the three servants knew something serious was about. Sarah had only seen Mrs. Norton that angry once—when the ham they'd served at a dinner party was a bit dry. Even then, she'd sent for them from the library.

Heads lowered, Ruth, Alice, and Sarah followed Mrs. Norton and Mrs. Owen down the long hall into the great room where the other house servants were somberly gathered. *What have we done?* wondered Sarah. The same question was mirrored on the other faces. Tension filled the room.

A wail sounded from upstairs. One of the children was sobbing loudly from grief. Although Sarah was concerned for the welfare of whatever child was in distress, she was also relieved. She'd never been allowed much contact with the children, so whatever trouble was happening couldn't involve her. She let out the breath she'd been unconsciously holding.

"Elizabeth's favorite doll is missing. Its glass case has been broken," said Mrs. Norton, facing the servants. "Do any of you know where it is?"

Sarah knew which doll Mistress Norton was talking about: the "Princess Victoria" doll, a delicate creation of china, satin, and fine artwork. A gift from a favorite aunt, thirteen-year-old Elizabeth had brought the doll to the table several times to show guests, immediately returning it to her room upstairs. A stab of guilt brought a flush to Sarah's cheeks. She'd coveted the doll every time she'd seen Elizabeth cradling it. Could whatever had happened be her fault in some way?

"I'm waiting for an answer." Anne Norton's voice was cold, but the veins standing out on her temples gave evidence of her immense wrath. She walked down the line of servants, searching each face.

Mrs. Norton was facing Ester, and though the maid's back was straight, her lips trembled at the intensity of her mistress's stare. Mrs. Norton moved on, seemingly convinced that Ester wasn't the guilty one.

No! Sarah's thoughts screamed as the woman came down the line toward her. *Don't let her look at me like that!* Standing next to her mother, Sarah tried to control her expression, but the more she willed her cheeks to stop burning, the hotter they felt.

"Sarah, look at me!"

Sarah brought her eyes up to face the woman in front of her, but the expression on her mistress's face terrified her. Cowered by the accusation in Mrs. Norton's eyes, Sarah lowered her own.

"Where did you put it, Sarah?" asked Mrs. Norton through clenched teeth.

"I. . .I didn't." She looked at her mother for help. "Mother, I didn't. . . ."

Ruth put her arm around her daughter, drawing her close. "Ma'am, the girl has always been truthful to me. She'd not be the type to—"

"Search her room!" snapped Mrs. Norton to Albert and Mrs. Owen.

Sarah felt her mother trembling against her. She wanted to reassure her that there was nothing to worry about, that she hadn't taken the doll, but the knowledge that the eyes of everyone in the room were upon her froze her tongue.

The next five minutes seemed like an eternity to Sarah. Hearing the footsteps of the returning servants, she looked up. Walking ahead of Albert, Mrs. Owen held the doll.

Sarah's mouth flew open, and she found her tongue. "No! I didn't take it!"

Mrs. Owen had always been kind to Sarah, and there was regret in her voice when she spoke. "It was under her bed, Madam, wrapped in her nightdress."

Closing her eyes, Sarah leaned her head against her mother's chest. "I didn't take the doll!" she sobbed, her shoulders heaving.

"Your daughter will have to leave," said Mrs. Norton, facing Ruth. "I'll have no thieves about here. You may stay, though. We've no complaints against you."

Ruth's head snapped back. "Ma'am, I ain't got a family to send her to, and I wouldn't if I had. Sarah's not a thief!" Humbling herself, she lowered her voice. "I've served you well these past fourteen years. Please don't do this to us."

Mrs. Norton frowned. "If you won't send her away, then your duties are no longer required in this household. Pack your things and have Ben drive you to town." Turning on her heel, she crossed the room, the doll in her arms.

"Oh, Missus Anne, please don't be so cruel," pleaded Ruth, taking a step forward as if to follow her employer.

Pausing at the first step of the staircase, Mrs. Norton put her hand on the banister rail and looked back, her face a mask of disdain. "Cruel? You dare to call me cruel, here in my own house and ahead of my servants? I should have known something like this would happen!" Her sharp voice dripped venom. "I've been too much of a lady to hold her breeding against her. I even gave her a home. But the ill-begotten will sooner or later seek their true level, won't they?"

Ashen-faced, Ruth put her hand over her heart, leaning on Sarah for support. Alice touched her shoulder. "I'll help you gather your things," she said quietly, her face a picture of ineffable sadness.

As they walked past the other servants, Sarah looked up at the sound of weeping. It lightened her heart a little to realize that they had some friends in the household. When she caught Celly's eyes she stopped short, confused at the message they were sending. Crossing her arms over her buxom chest, the red-haired maid grinned broadly.

four
1836

"Remember to stand up straight, Sarah," said Ruth, holding open the wrought-iron gate leading to the great house.

When Connelsworth Park first came into their sights, Sarah had only been able to stare at the majesty of it. Now she found her tongue. "Mother, are you sure we should apply here? Mrs. Norton said that—"

"Lower your voice, child! You'll have us turned away before we get inside the door!"

Sarah wanted to obey, but she found herself faltering. "Mrs. Norton said that Mrs. Gerty—she's crazy! I heard the Mistress and her friends talking about her lots of times!"

Shifting the roll of clothing and belongings she carried to her other arm, Ruth took Sarah's elbow, pulling gently to hurry her along as they followed a cobbled path to the back of the house. "We've nowhere else to look," she whispered. "And our savings is almost gone."

"But there must be some—"

Stopping a few feet from the door, Ruth wheeled her daughter around to face her. "I don't like to talk ugly about the mistress, even if she did send us away, but her and her friends wasn't kind when they talked about people. Mrs. Gerty can't be as bad as they said."

She took the smaller bundle from under Sarah's arm and set it down in the grass growing near the path. "Now, let's brush the dirt from our dresses and wipe the sweat off your face with this handkerchief. We want to look presentable, don't we?"

Swallowing hard, Sarah nodded. "What if she won't hire

us? Mrs. Norton might have told her about us, too." They'd found when they'd begun seeking other employment that Mrs. Norton had spread word among her friends that Ruth and Sarah were insolent and dishonest. Even potential employers who weren't acquainted with the Nortons wouldn't consider them without a letter of recommendation.

"We've got to try, little Sarah. That's all there is to it," Ruth said, bending to pick up their bundles again. Stepping up to the wooden door, she pulled the rope on a large brass bell affixed to the frame.

After a while the knob turned, and the door was pulled open by a ruddy-faced woman wearing a smeared white apron, obviously the cook or kitchen maid.

Eyeing the bundles they were holding, the woman shook her head. "We don't need nothin' today," she said, not unkindly. The door was starting to swing shut when Ruth put out her hand to catch it. "We're not selling, ma'am. We're seeking jobs."

The woman at the door laughed, then darted a look behind her. "Are you that desperate?"

"Yes."

"Do you have a wagon waiting in front?"

"No, ma'am. We walked here."

Her eyebrows shot up. "All the way from town in this muggy weather?"

Ruth nodded.

"Then you must be desperate indeed! Let me send for Miss Martin. She's the housekeeper. You can wait in the kitchen."

They followed her through a short hallway, then down a flight of stone steps. Sarah had heard of underground kitchens, but she'd never been in one. She was astounded at the coolness of the room, a welcome relief from the oppressive heat they'd walked in all morning.

Setting out from the far wall was a huge cooking range with ovens on either side of its coal grate. From hooks on the brick wall hung a multitude of iron and copper sauce pans, skillets, skimmers, and sieves. The shelves covering another wall were stacked with fancy pudding molds, jelly and aspic dishes, preserving pans, bread tins, milk bowls, and numerous other utensils. Some she'd never seen before, even though she'd been raised in a kitchen.

Ruth, turning around to take it all in, let out a sigh. "The size of this kitchen!" she said. "It's twice as big as what I'm used to!"

"All the rooms are big, dear," said the woman. "Except the servants' rooms, of course." She turned to a girl about Sarah's age who was at a table peeling beets. "Frances, go ask Miss Martin to come."

The girl put her knife down and got up from the table. Wiping her hands on her apron, she gave Sarah a shy smile before trotting up the stairway and through the door at the top.

"My name is Agnes. I'm the cook. Would you be wantin' to put your bundles down?" Pulling out a chair, she motioned for them to put their belongings on it. "You look like you could use some water, too."

"Thank you for your kindness," said Ruth as she laid their things in the chair. "Have you worked here long?"

"Five years," answered Agnes, dipping two tin mugs in a bucket on the sideboard. "Longer than anyone else, 'cept for Miss Martin. Folks with any sense don't stay around here very long."

Ruth was opening her mouth to question this statement when the door at the head of the stairs opened again. In walked a stick of a woman.

Sarah's eyes grew wide. She'd never seen anyone that thin! The fullness of the woman's black skirt and white starched apron only made her arms and torso seem more skeletal. Her sparse, dull brown hair was pulled back tightly into a bun at the nape of her neck, drawing attention to her colorless sunken cheeks and severe lips.

"You are looking for positions, I'm told," she said, still standing at the top of the stairs. "May I see your letter of reference?"

"We got no letter, ma'am," said Ruth. "But my daughter and I—"

"I'm afraid Mrs. Gerty requires a reference," interrupted Miss Martin. "You may leave now."

"Do you mind if I give them a bite to eat first?" asked Agnes quickly. "They walked all the way from town."

"Hand them a loaf of bread and get on with your duties," Miss Martin answered as she turned back to the door.

"Please tell the mistress that we was fired by Mrs. Henry Norton," Ruth spoke out to the woman's back.

Miss Martin paused at the door, her hand on the knob. "Fired?"

"Yes, and wrongly too."

She turned to look at them, then shrugged. "That still doesn't—"

Ruth bit her lip, her face anxious. "Please tell her that we don't believe none of the horrible things Mrs. Norton said about her."

Miss Martin stared at them. Then, to Sarah's amazement, a corner of the housekeeper's mouth twitched.

As if embarrassed by this faint show of emotion, Miss Martin straightened her bony shoulders. "You may give them something to eat," she said to Agnes, without looking at Sarah and Ruth. "I shall see if the mistress would like to speak with them."

"I believe Miss Martin was about to smile!" said Agnes, shaking her head in wonder. She handed Sarah a soft roll, smeared with meat paste. "I'd have thought a corpse more likely to!"

"She does seem a sad one," said Ruth.

"Sad? That would take some feelings. The woman's got a stone for a heart—and a wee one at that!"

Sarah watched Frances peeling beets. She longed to speak to the girl, but the unfamiliar surroundings intimidated her. As if reading her thoughts, Frances looked up from the basket in her lap.

"I hope you can stay," she said. "Ginny is the nearest one to my age, and she's three years older than me."

"I hope so, too," Sarah replied. *Mother's right,* she thought. *Mrs. Norton said bad things about lots of people.* While it was true that Miss Martin was a bit cold, Sarah liked the idea of having a friend her age. Maybe she and her mother could be happy working in the house, even if Mrs. Gerty was odd.

The kitchen door swung open. "Mrs. Gerty would like to see you in the sitting room," said Miss Martin, her face expressionless.

Rising from their chairs, Ruth and Sarah silently followed her up the steps and down a short passageway, through a huge dining room, and down a second, longer hall. When they came to a door near the end of this hall, Miss Martin knocked softly.

A high voice called out. "You may come in."

Miss Martin opened the door and motioned for them to go inside.

"You stay here, too, Julia, so they aren't wandering around the house when they leave."

When they leave! In her disappointment, Sarah forgot to hold her back straight as she followed her mother and Miss

Martin through the doorway. The sitting room was massive, with paintings of all sorts lining the walls. Burgundy velvet curtains hung at the windows, and brilliantly colored carpets nearly covered the polished floor.

As big as the room was, it was crammed almost to bursting with furniture. Damask and striped silk sofas, armchairs, a variety of little tables and cabinets, reading stands, embroidered footstools, and carved bookcases stood about in profusion, and in the corner stood a stately grand piano.

Remembering why they were visiting, Sarah straightened her back and walked from behind her mother to stand next to her. Seated in front of them was a short, stout woman. Her pink silk dress, with its rows of ruffles, silk bows, and tiny wreaths of rosebuds, was designed for someone much younger.

"What did Mrs. Norton say about me?" Mrs. Gerty demanded of Ruth. A row of flesh bubbled out from under her chin when she spoke. "Tell me everything!"

Closing her eyes, Ruth struggled with herself. Then she reached for her daughter's hand and squeezed it. "She said you was crazy."

"Crazy!" The mass of ringlets in Mrs. Gerty's graying black hair quivered, and her body shook with rage. "She's got some nerve calling me crazy!" Narrowing her small eyes, she asked, "Who did she say this to?"

Sarah could hear her mother gulp. "I heard her say it to Mrs. Waldsworth, Miss Farington, and Mrs. Helen Smith, among others."

"Do you think they believe her?" asked Mrs. Gerty. Her fleshy, pallid cheeks were covered with angry red splotches, and Sarah was shaken at the utter hatred in her eyes, even though it was not directed at them.

"Mrs. Norton talks bad about a lot of people," answered

Ruth. "Only a simpleton would believe her gossip. Why, she accused my daughter of being a thief!"

Sarah looked up at her mother, not believing her ears! They'd had too many prospective employers throw that up at them, for most well-connected people around Bristol knew the Nortons. And now Mother was volunteering the information!

"Well, maybe she is a thief!" snorted Mrs. Gerty, sharply eyeing Sarah's terrified face.

"Another maid in the house has boasted to our friends that she stole a doll and hid it under my daughter's bed. When we found out, we tried to see Mrs. Norton, but she won't see us or change her mind, even though she fired the other maid a few days after we left."

While Mrs. Gerty considered her words, Ruth pressed on. "She's told everyone in town that she won't speak to anyone who hires us. We came here, ma'am, because we figure you ain't one to be told what to do."

"You're right about that!" said Mrs. Gerty. "I'll not be having the likes of Anne Norton telling me who I can or cannot hire!"

Ruth squeezed Sarah's hand again. "Then would you have a position for us? We was in the kitchen at the house, but we can do other work besides."

Mrs. Gerty reached for an almond-shaped chocolate from a dish on the settee and popped it into her plump mouth. After chewing with obvious relish, she licked her lips. "I have one position open, for the girl."

Sarah and her mother looked at each other.

"I don't like having lots of servants around," continued Mrs. Gerty, a flake of chocolate still at the corner of her mouth. "I have to feed and pay them all, and they get lazy when there's not enough work to keep them busy."

"Ma'am," said Ruth, stepping forward. "The child's not used to drawing a salary, so's if we could stay together, you'd only have to pay me."

"I don't think so. Sooner or later, you'd get to grumbling about it and walk around here with a sour face. I expect my servants to look pleasant."

Sarah couldn't help but glance at Miss Martin, who looked anything but pleasant!

Ruth pressed on, an edge of panic in her voice. "We didn't grumble at the Nortons', and we'd be grateful to you if we could have a place here."

"Food isn't free around here," answered Mrs. Gerty, "and I presume you'd want to eat. No, the girl is enough, or both of you take your leave and I'll hire someone else."

"Then, you'll take on my Sarah?"

"That would suit me fine. I'll pay four shillings a month, as I can't be expected to give full wages for a child. How old is she—ten?"

"She's thirteen, ma'am, and a hard worker."

"We'll see." Mrs. Gerty reached for another chocolate. "Miss Martin, show her where she'll sleep tonight and give her something to do."

Numb, Sarah walked with her mother and Miss Martin back down the long hallway and up two flights of stairs to a tiny, windowless attic room. She didn't speak until the housekeeper left them alone.

"Mother," she sobbed, throwing her arms around her waist. "I don't want to stay here without you!"

Gathering her daughter in her arms, Ruth sat on the flock mattress on the bed. "My child, it tears my heart out to leave you, but right now you need a place to stay."

"You need a place, too! Where will you stay?"

"I heard a woman in the rooming-house say they're hiring workers at the cotton mill. I can get a job and bed there until something better comes along. Then I can come get you."

Sarah's head shot up. "I can get a job there, too, and we can be together."

"No!" Ruth's voice was firm. "I'll never have you working in one of them places! No matter how hard you have to work, you'll have it better here than the little ones in the factories!"

Gently setting Sarah down from her lap onto the mattress, Ruth rose. "I'd best be going now, so's I can reach town before dark."

Dumb with anguish, Sarah could only reach out for a handful of her mother's skirt. Like in the old days, she held the fold of limp broadcloth to her cheek, her eyes closed.

Ruth stood for a while, her hand resting on her daughter's head. "Oh, child," she finally groaned, "this ain't forever. I'll come to see you when I can." After carefully untangling Sarah's fingers from her skirt, she bent down and kissed her forehead. "You hang on to your wages. Find a safe place. When we've got enough saved, you and me, we'll go to another town and look for positions where they never heard of Mrs. Norton!" Giving Sarah one last, quick hug, she was gone.

A soft rap sounded at Sarah's door. Rising from where she'd thrown herself on the bed, Sarah wiped her eyes. "Come in," she said hesitantly, fearful of who might be on the other side.

A pretty, golden-haired girl of about fifteen came in, holding Sarah's belongings and some folded linens. "I brought you some sheets and your bundle. There's a blanket in the bottom of the chest." She eyed Sarah. "Well, you're a wee one, like Frances. You'd best dry up them tears before the missus sees you."

"Are you Ginny?" asked Sarah.

"A smart one, too, I see! That's me name, for certain. I'm the parlor maid. How old are you?"

"Thirteen."

"The same age I was when I came on," said Ginny. "The missus likes to hire 'em young 'cause we don't eat much, and so's she can pay half-wages. The only thing is, when you get older, she forgets to raise the pay." Handing Sarah a coarse cotton sheet, she turned and fetched a brown woolen blanket from the chest. "I'll help you make your bed if you'll stop standing there like you ain't got any sense."

Positioning herself at the foot of the bed, Sarah helped Ginny tuck the sheet in around the mattress. "Why don't you get a position somewhere else?" she finally asked.

"When's a body supposed to look for work? I've had only three days off since I came here—one to go to my aunt's funeral, and two more when I was taken ill." She frowned. "I get a half-day every month, but Mrs. Gerty won't let Alex drive me to town in the wagon. By the time I walked there, it'd be time to turn around and come back!"

"My mother used to have half-Sundays off every week," said Sarah, warming up to the talkative older girl. "She was a cook."

"Well, no wonder about that. Agnes gets half-Sundays off, too. Good cooks are hard to find, I hear, so's they get treated a mite better."

Sometimes they are, thought Sarah. *But not always.*

"Now," said Ginny, smoothing out the last wrinkle in the blanket. "Miss Martin says you've had your lunch, and I'm to show you what to do." She motioned for Sarah to follow her. "Most important," she said as they started down the dark attic stairs, "is to stay busy. And when you see the missus, you'd best look happy. Even if you ain't."

Finished! thought Sarah, squeezing the rags she'd used to clean the billiard room fireplace. Ginny had taught her to scour the iron grate with vinegar and sand from a bucket in the tool shed. It seemed a waste to clean it when the morning fires would be laid in less than an hour, but Sarah knew better than to question an order.

Her right shoulder ached from scrubbing, but she didn't ache all over anymore. After six months at Mrs. Gerty's, her body was getting used to hard work. She looked down at her hands. They were red and coarse not only from the continual scrubbing and polishing, but also from the strong lye in the laundry soap.

It wouldn't be so bad if her mother were working with her. The ache in her chest was far worse than the pain in her shoulder, and the loneliness far worse than the drudgery. Frances spent all her time in the kitchen helping Agnes. Even though their rooms were next door to each other, they rarely had time to talk. At the end of each day it was all they could do to pull themselves up the attic stairs and fall into bed, sometimes without even pulling down the sheets.

Mealtimes in the kitchen—the bright spots in Sarah's day—were rushed, and if a maid wanted enough to eat, she'd best spend that time eating instead of talking.

Suddenly, Sarah's thoughts turned to panic. *What am I doing, just sitting here!* Holding her breath, she listened. The room was quiet. Slowly, she turned her head to the left, examining the shadowy spots out of the corner of her eye.

She let out a breath and reached for the crock of vinegar and wet rags. Rising, she looked one last time around the room, careful to keep a smile on her face.

five
1838-1840

"You learn a lot by keepin' your ears open," advised Ginny, picking up the bread crumbs that were left on her plate with her fingers. " 'Stead of going around with your head in the clouds."

Sarah blushed, but Ginny's wink told her the older girl wasn't being unkind. The female servants were taking their time at breakfast. Miss Martin had left early for Bristol to purchase household goods, and Mrs. Gerty hadn't rung her bell for breakfast. They'd have to rush through chores at an even greater speed, but the relaxed companionship was worth it.

"So, what have you learned, m'lady?" asked Agnes, resting her elbows on the table.

"I found out how come the mister and missus is so rich."

Sarah remembered that she'd overheard Mrs. Norton and her friends tittering over how the Gertys had acquired their immense wealth, but she couldn't recall the details. That life had been over a year ago and seemed like a dream.

Pleased at having her audience so attentive, Ginny continued. "Alex told me that Leslie, that new gardener, told him they wasn't always rich. I mean, they wasn't as poor as the likes of us, but Mr. Gerty was a clerk in the shipping business, or somewhat like that."

Agnes sat up straight, a mock look of horror on her face. "You mean they ain't gentlefolk?"

"In a sow's eye!" Their giggles of delight caused Sarah to glance at the stairs. She couldn't believe they were talking this way!

"Anyhow, Leslie says he heard Mr. Gerty leased a ship and made buckets of money haulin' slaves 'cross the ocean—even after it was against the law."

Frances's eyes grew wide. "He sold little black babies?"

"Right out of their mommies' arms. Course he sold some grown ones, too."

"That's horrible!" exclaimed Sarah. "Is he still doing it?"

"No, that was a long time ago. But he made enough money to start his own shipping business and to buy this here house." Ginny leaned closer to the table. "I heard they bought it from some gentry that had more land than sense, and the mister and missus gave them a tenth of what it's worth!"

Bringing her dish and mug to the washbasin, Sarah felt keen disappointment in Mr. Gerty, though she barely knew him. He stayed mostly at a club in Bristol, close to his business. Of course, she thought grimly, she couldn't blame Mr. Gerty for staying away, even if he had sold slaves once.

"My, ain't we jumpy these days!" said Agnes, who'd brushed against Sarah on her way to the basin.

Sarah looked down at her broken dish on the floor. "I'm so sorry!"

After helping Sarah throw the broken pieces away, Agnes put an arm around the girl's shoulders and gave her a squeeze. "You can't let the missus upset you so," she whispered, "or you'll end up as daffy as she!"

Sarah would have liked to have stayed enveloped in Agnes's plump arms. It had been so long since she'd seen her mother. When the cook finally turned away to give her attention to the dishes, Frances touched Sarah's arm. "Are you all right?"

She nodded, managing a little smile. *Poor Frances,* she thought. *At least I have a mother who'll come for me one day.* Frances had been recruited from an orphanage and knew nothing about her parentage.

Mrs. Gerty still wasn't up, so Sarah couldn't carry down the chamber pots. She reached into her apron pocket and brought out her list of duties for the day—cleaning the drawing room was next. Miss Martin had given her a list of duties for every day of the week, but Sarah had been too embarrassed to tell the housekeeper that the marks on the page meant nothing to her. Fortunately, Ginny was able to read them to her, and within a month's time, she knew what the words stood for.

Sarah brought a handful of clean rags and a jar of linseed oil into the drawing room and cleared the knick-knacks from the rosewood table nearest the door. First, the table had to be rubbed with a dab of linseed oil on a soft cloth, then buffed with a piece of lamb's wool. After the polishing was done, Sarah dusted the ornamental vase, candlestick, china figurines, and glass dome of wax flowers.

Well, that one's finished, she thought, looking around the room. She let out a sigh, for knick-knacks abounded on every surface. Why not close up the rooms that were never used and cover the furniture with sheets? Mrs. Gerty never entertained guests, yet she demanded that every room in the house be kept spotless.

"What's the matter? Don't you have enough to do?"

Sarah jumped at the familiar voice. To her right was Mrs. Gerty, her head showing from where she was crouched behind an overstuffed sofa.

"You thought I was still asleep, didn't you? Figured you'd dawdle without Miss Martin around to make sure you do your work!"

"No, ma'am, not at all. I was just—"

Standing and making her way around the sofa, Mrs. Gerty shook a pudgy finger at the girl. "You were just stealing from me, that's what you were doing! I pay good wages in exchange for your services, but you idle about!"

Sarah knew that there was no use arguing. "Yes, ma'am," she whispered, hanging her head.

"You think it was you that was crowned last year instead of Princess Victoria, is that it? Do you want to be Queen of England?" Mrs. Gerty stepped closer, hovering over the girl so that Sarah could feel her sour breath on her forehead. "Does your highness have better things to do than earn your keep?"

"No, ma'am."

"Look at me when I speak to you, you ugly wretch! Do you know that there's a cellar under this room with a big, heavy door?"

Paling, Sarah looked at Mrs. Gerty as commanded. "Yes, ma'am."

"How would you like to spend a few days down there with rats and spiders crawling all over you?"

"Please—"

"Please, what? You filthy little beast!" Mrs. Gerty drew back her teeth in a grin, enjoying Sarah's terror. "I could come down there with a big knife and rip your stomach open. Wouldn't the creatures down there love to gobble your innards!"

Don't faint. It'll be over soon, Sarah told herself, biting her lower lip as she kept her eyes on Mrs. Gerty's.

"No one would ever know." Mrs. Gerty's voice was lower, more sinister. "Perhaps I've done it before to other lazy girls, and do you see me in prison? I'd tell anyone who cared enough to come looking for a nothing like you that you stole money and ran off!

"And there you'd be, beneath their very feet, a pile of chewed-up bones! Do you think the constable would dispute my word? I'd tell him, 'I don't wish to press charges if you find the poor creature. She's suffered enough already.' And I'd look so worried about you—even wipe a tear from my eye!"

Mrs. Gerty brought her face inches from Sarah's. "I might have mercy on you this time—though you surely don't deserve it—and hold back this month's salary. But next time, I may choose something more effective!"

"Yes, ma'am," said Sarah, her forehead beaded with sweat.

"Is that all you can say, you ingrate?"

"I mean thank you, ma'am."

"Say it like you mean it!"

Sarah stretched her lips into a smile. "Thank you, ma'am."

Mrs. Gerty narrowed her eyes. "Am I going to see you sulking about, or will you manage to look agreeable?"

The smile still frozen on her face, Sarah answered. "I plan to look pleasant, ma'am."

Sarah was carrying an armload of folded sheets up the back stairway when Miss Martin called from the foot of the stairs. Turning around, Sarah wondered if she'd done anything wrong.

"Sarah, after you put those in the linen-closet, you may visit your guest in the kitchen."

Sarah nearly dropped the sheets she was holding. "Do you mean my mother?"

Miss Martin nodded, her face impassive. "You may take your half-day off today instead of waiting until Thursday."

"Oh, thank you, Miss Martin!" Sarah flew halfway down the steps before she remembered the bundle in her arms. "Oh, the sheets!" she said, tearing back up the staircase.

It only took a few seconds for Sarah to put the sheets away and head for the kitchen. Bursting through the door, she cried out, "Mother!"

Suddenly, those arms she'd longed for were wrapped around her. "I missed you so, my little Sarah," said Ruth.

"Oh, Mother. I thought I would die for wanting to see you!" Sarah said.

After a while, Ruth put her hands on her daughter's shoulders and took a step back. "Mercy, child, I believe you've grown!"

For the first time in almost two years, Sarah got a good look at her mother. Her face was sallow. Wrinkles creased her forehead. A deep cough racked her body with violent heaves.

"Sit here, Miss Ruth," offered Agnes, coming over from the stove and pulling out a chair. "You sound like you're coming down with croup."

"No, it's not that," Ruth said, lowering herself in the chair. "It's my lungs—the cotton mill."

Agnes nodded. "I've heard about such things. It's a shame you couldn't find another position as cook."

"Heard about what things?" asked Sarah, alarmed. "Are you dying?"

"No, of course not," reassured her mother. "I'm just—" Her words were interrupted by another fit of coughing.

When the coughing had eased, Ruth took a sip from the steaming cup of tea Frances put in front of her. "Thank you, child." She smiled tenderly at Frances, and some of her former beauty shone through.

"It's the cotton fibers. They float around us while we work. I've taken to keeping a cloth tied around my mouth and nose, and I expect that'll help a lot—as soon as this cough clears up."

Sarah caught the look that passed over Agnes's face, though the cook quickly smiled and started bustling around. "Mother,

I don't want you to work there anymore!" Sarah insisted. "It's been over two years since we left the Nortons'. I know you can find a better position now!"

Ruth shook her head. "Nobody'd hire me. They'd be scared I've got somethin' contagious." She reached for her daughter's hand. "I'm afraid I've had to spend most of my savings at the doctor's. But I'll get better soon and start savin' again. Can you wait a little longer?"

Behind her mother's back, Agnes gave Sarah a meaningful look.

"Yes, Mother. I'll wait."

Beaming, Ruth reached across the table for her hand. "I feel better! I was so worried when I left you here, I could hardly sleep nights for cryin'. It's good to see you've got friends here. You're happy, ain't you?"

"Yes," Sarah lied. "Everyone is kind to me."

Before Sarah knew it, her mother had to leave. "They gave us a whole day off 'cause Mr. Johnson's getting married—he owns the mill. But it'll be dark soon, and I should've started back a while ago. I wanted to be with you as long as I could."

"Alex will drive you back in the wagon," came Miss Martin's voice from the top of the kitchen stairs. "I've decided we need some silver-polish from town." Knowing that Alex couldn't possibly find a shop open, Sarah shot Miss Martin a grateful look.

The wagon was out of sight when Sarah stopped waving. She was glad she'd fetched the coins she'd saved and pressed them in her mother's hand—two years' wages.

Four months later, Agnes came up to Sarah's room where the girl was making her bed.

"She's gone, dear child. Pneumonia."

Brush and dustpan in hand, Sarah paused outside the door

to the library, checking her apron pocket for matches to light the oil lamps. The carpets in the library were too heavy to carry outside and had to be brushed by hand. Now that she was fifteen, she performed her tasks mechanically, looking forward to when she could retire at night for a few hours of blessed unconsciousness. *I'll never be able to leave,* she thought.

Pushing the door open, Sarah was surprised to see a low light coming from one of the lamps near the settee. She thought Mrs. Gerty had come to scream at her until she realized that the person seated was Miss Martin.

"I'm sorry," Sarah said. "Do you want me to clean the carpets later?"

"No, I'll leave," Miss Martin said, not moving. Her voice was unsteady, and Sarah wondered if the housekeeper had been crying.

"Miss Martin?" she said. "Are you all right?"

"No."

Sarah didn't know what to say. She walked tentatively across the room and stood a few feet away from the woman. "Can I help? You look ill."

Miss Martin smiled bitterly. "Ill? Yes, that's it. Only it's my heart that's ill."

"You're unhappy?" The thought was new to Sarah. She'd assumed that Miss Martin had no emotions. Even after the housekeeper had been so kind that day her mother had visited, she'd remained aloof, speaking to Sarah only when there was a duty to assign.

"Please, come sit with me," said Miss Martin. "I'll help you clean the carpets later so you won't fall behind."

Taking a seat on the settee, Sarah glanced timidly at the woman. Miss Martin's face was splotched, her eyes swollen.

"Sometimes I have a spell of feeling sorry for my state," Miss Martin finally said. "I haven't cried about it for a long time, but this morning I felt overwhelmed." She turned to Sarah. "You must find a way to leave here," she said, her voice suddenly stronger, determined, "or you'll end up like me—bound here for life!"

"I'm saving my wages so's I can go somewhere else and look for work. It's just taking a while."

"You'll never have enough if Mrs. Gerty has anything to do with it! And do you think she'd give you a reference if you told her you were leaving?"

"Is that why you've never left?"

Miss Martin pointed to a painting next to a bookcase. A boy of about seven years stood behind the chair where a girl, perhaps two or three years younger, sat. The boy had his hands on the girl's shoulders, and while their expressions were serious, they both looked healthy.

"My brother and I," said Miss Martin. "We were born in this house."

Sarah's mouth dropped open. "You?"

"As was our father before us. We had servants everywhere and visitors calling. When I was fifteen or so, my mother hired a serving maid my age, a Helen Andrews. She was a quiet girl and pretty—and quite smitten by my brother, James."

Miss Martin looked up at the portrait again. "James had an eye for the ladies, but he seemed to pay the servant girls no mind." Turning back to Sarah, she said, "We were disappointed when James failed at Oxford, but Mother was determined that he should marry well."

"And did he marry?"

"Never. Neither did I, though I was engaged. After my brother returned from college, Mother's maid told her that

James had been seen on the servant's stairway late at night and early in the mornings. Mother inquired further and discharged Helen from her position."

Sarah didn't understand where all this was leading, but she nodded anyway.

"Helen didn't take it too well. She cursed my mother, saying that James had promised to marry her. I had never heard such profanity. And the terrible things she threatened to do to our family! James denied any such promise. He went away on holiday that same day with some friends.

"My mother and father had us children in their later years," Miss Martin continued. "They passed away within six months of each other when I was twenty-three. Four years later I was engaged to marry a dashing young man."

Miss Martin smiled and clasped her hands to her sunken chest, looking past Sarah with shining eyes. "I'd always been plain, but he told me I was beautiful! He made plans about what we'd do after we were married, and I was swept off my feet!

"Three months before our wedding, James died in a drunken brawl. Our solicitor went over the family finances and discovered that we were deeply in debt." Miss Martin shook her head. "James had squandered away a fortune."

New tears were forming in Miss Martin's eyes, and Sarah tentatively reached for her hand.

"When I told my husband-to-be the news, he bowed out of the engagement. One year later he married another plain, wealthy girl. Our family solicitor arranged to put our home up for sale, and the man who bought it paid off my debts. I was left penniless. I've always wondered if my attorney had been dishonest, especially after I heard that he had gone into business with the man who bought my house."

A bitter smile came to Miss Martin's lips. "The man's wife

kindly suggested I stay here until I found a position at a girls' school. I would be expected to earn my keep as the house-keeper."

Sarah's eyebrows drew together. "I don't understand. Why did you stay as a servant when you could have done something else?"

"I regret it so much, Sarah, but my life had been sheltered. I was always a shy person, and the rejection by my suitor left me more timid than ever and ashamed to face people. I told myself that I would leave when the right position came along."

Suddenly, it dawned on Sarah. "The serving maid that your family fired?"

"Helen Gerty became her married name."

They were both quiet. Sarah broke the silence. "You can still leave, Miss Martin. Haven't you any money saved up after all these years?"

Miss Martin shook her head. "I'm too old. No, I'll die here one day, under that woman's thumb."

Sarah was helping Frances scrub the pantry floor when Miss Martin entered. It had been almost a year since Sarah had had the talk with the housekeeper in the drawing room. She felt affection for her, though the woman was still tight-lipped.

"Madam would like you to wax the dining room floor again. She is having a guest tomorrow. An American woman, I'm told."

Frances's eyebrows shot up. "Somebody came from across the ocean to see the missus?"

"The lady's husband, a Mr. Carlton, is transacting some business with Mr. Gerty. Mrs. Gerty offered to entertain Mrs. Carlton."

A guest! Even though it meant more work, a change from
the routine was welcome. Since Ginny was no longer here—
she'd married Leslie, the gardener, six months earlier and
they'd found positions elsewhere—Sarah would be helping
Frances serve the noon meal.

The next day, Miss Martin caught Sarah's arm as she was
returning to the dining room with a tray of dessert pies.

"Did you hear what the lady said about wishing for an
English maid?" She squeezed Sarah's arm. "This is your
chance. You must catch her out front when she leaves!"

"But what if—"

"Do you want to stay here forever?"

Sarah bit her lip. "Mrs. Gerty will be—"

"I'll try to call her attention to something upstairs when the
lady leaves the front door. Take the chance, Sarah—and
Godspeed!"

six
1840

"Now, we're leaving Bristol to go back to the States in two days. Meet us at the dock, and I'm sure we'll have your passage ready. Should I send a carriage for you?"

"Could I come with you now?" asked Sarah, fearful that Mrs. Carlton would change her mind if pressed too hard, but more afraid of facing Mrs. Gerty.

Mrs. Carlton studied Sarah's face for a few seconds. "How old are you, dear?"

"Sixteen, ma'am."

"Are things so bad here?"

"Yes'm," Sarah cried, embarrassed by the tears that gathered in her eyes. "I can't go back, not now!"

"Well, climb on in then!" Mrs. Carlton said.

"You mean, you were born and raised in Bristol, and you've never seen a ship?" Amos Carlton laughed at the expression on Sarah's face when Bristol Harbor came into view. "Do they look like you imagined?"

Reverently, Sarah shook her head. "I seen pictures hangin' on the walls at the house, but I didn't know they was this big!"

She sat up straight in the open carriage so she could take in as much as possible. A few yards beyond the stone quay was blue-green water, speckled with whitecaps. White sails flickered in the sunlight as coastal schooners and brigs picked their way through the channel leading to the Severn estuary.

"There's our ship," said Mr. Carlton, pointing. "The *Eastern Star.*"

Nearly six-hundred feet long, the ship had four smoking chimneys and a thirty-foot-high wall of black iron punched through by portholes. Six masts, tall as trees, rose from her decks, with enough canvas to bed a small town.

Most captivating to Sarah's eyes was the bow, where a carved woman with the body of a fish held both arms out as if to embrace the sea. On each side of the woman were dolphins, their bodies painted so that they looked cast in bronze.

As their carriage came closer to the dock, even Mr. Carlton let out a low whistle. "Well, she's the finest ship I've ever set eyes upon! They say we'll be back in the States in about three weeks if the weather cooperates." He shook his gray head. "Steam engines! When my present contracts expire, I want to ship all the company's merchandise this way. Just think of—"

"When your contracts expire?" Mrs. Carlton, seated next to her husband, looked puzzled. "Haven't you made an agreement with Mr. Gerty about your next shipping arrangements?"

Mr. Carlton cleared his throat. "I didn't sign with Gerty, though his pricing was quite competitive. I meant to tell you yesterday, but when you came back to the hotel with the little lady here, it slipped my mind."

"Slipped your mind! We came all the way across the Atlantic—"

"Now, Mary," he said, "I could have sent Wesley to handle this, but you said you wanted to see Europe before you got too old to travel. Seems to me we got our money's worth out of this trip."

"Yes, it's been enjoyable." Mrs. Carlton tilted her head in Sarah's direction. "Even interesting. But why did you change your plans?"

"Something told me not to trust the man. He and his lawyer seemed too pushy, and when I looked over the contracts, I found some changes—"

"You don't have to explain," said his wife, reaching over and patting his hand. "You've built a successful business by trusting your instincts, and I'm not going to question them now."

Mr. Carlton grinned, the laughlines deep at the corners of his eyes. "I guess not after your instincts told you to kidnap that lady's maid!"

"My dear, it wasn't kidnapping, and that was no lady!"

At the pier, the three joined a dozen or so other people on board a harbor-taxi to be ferried out to the *Eastern Star*.

After the stewards carried the trunks to their stateroom, Sarah helped Mrs. Carlton unpack while Mr. Carlton went up on deck. Mrs. Carlton looked through the small doorway leading to Sarah's tiny berth. "It's rather small," she said, "but it's only for three weeks."

"Oh, ma'am," Sarah exclaimed, "it's only a little tinier than my room in the attic. I can't thank you enough for taking me on!"

"You're welcome. I'm sure you'll perform your duties diligently." The older woman closed her eyes. "It may be that your first duties will be quite unpleasant. I became horribly seasick on our trip over. Amos has assured me that the ship's great speed will lessen the pitching and tossing, but I'm afraid I'm feeling queasy even now."

Sarah hadn't noticed before, but the floor was moving, a subtle, rocking motion, even though the ship was in dock.

"Perhaps you should lie down a bit, ma'am," said Sarah. When Mrs. Carlton nodded, her eyes still closed, Sarah pulled down the covers and guided her by the elbow over to the bed.

"I ain't ever taken care of anyone with the seasickness," she said softly as she tucked the comforter around the lady. "Is there anything else I should do?"

"Yes," groaned Mrs. Carlton. "Pull that rope next to you and call for a steward. Ask for some arrowroot. And a bucket."

One week into the journey, Mrs. Carlton hadn't been able to leave her bed save for short walks on deck propped between her husband and Sarah. "The fresh air will do you good," her husband would tell her, coaxing her out of bed.

After four days, Mrs. Carlton flatly refused to try. "The effort is too great, and it doesn't make me feel better," she said weakly. "I was hoping this trip would be easier than the one over. I wish we'd stayed home!"

It's so beautiful, the ocean, thought Sarah, taking an appreciative whiff of salt breeze as she carried a bucket out on deck. She felt so sorry for Mrs. Carlton, who was unable to appreciate the deep blue of the water or the hazy, fine-spun clouds that pillowed the sky.

Pinching a piece from the soft bread roll in her pocket, Sarah put it in her mouth and chewed. Mr. Carlton had advised her to keep something in her stomach at all times. So far she'd been able to keep the bread down, though the slight nausea was constant.

She was emptying the contents of the bucket over the railing when the skin on the inside of her thumb got pinched between the bucket and the wire handle.

"Ouch!" she cried out, jerking her hand away. In an instant, the pail flew out of her reach. She leaned over the rail, trying to catch the lost bucket.

"Hey, that's not a wise thing to do!" Sarah felt a hand on her arm. A sandy-haired young man, only an inch or so taller than her, was at her right. "You don't want to drown because of a bucket!" he said in an American accent.

"I wasn't thinking," said Sarah, straightening. She gave the man an embarrassed smile. "Thank you for your concern."

"Of course," he said. When he returned her smile, his eyes lit up, making his rather plain features almost handsome. "I'd hate to have you fall overboard right in front of me—especially when I can't swim. Would you like another bucket?"

"Oh dear," said Sarah, glancing toward the water where the bucket disappeared. "I can't take yours."

"Please." Pulling the top bucket from a stack under his arm, he handed it to her. "This ship was prepared to hold two-hundred people, but only eighty or so are on board, so there're plenty of supplies." Looking up at the funnels at the stern, he shook his head. "People don't quite trust the steamers yet, but they're the wave of the future."

"Do you work on the ship?"

He flashed a boyish grin. "I just like ships. Actually, some families down in steerage are seasick, and there's no one to care for them. I'm helping out."

Bidding her good-day, he turned and headed for a passageway. Before he reached the door, he turned around.

"What's your name?" he called out.

"It's Sarah."

"Sarah," he repeated as he disappeared through the doorway. Sarah hurried back to the Carltons' room.

"I'm sorry I took so long, but I lost—"

Mr. Carlton put his finger to his lips. "She hasn't needed it," he whispered. "She fell asleep soon after you left." He reached over and, with thumb and forefinger, moved a tendril of gray hair from his wife's cheek.

"I'll watch her now if you'd like to get some air," Sarah said softly, touched by his devotion.

"No, I'm a bit tired. I think I'll have a rest myself. Why don't you go explore the ship? You've spent most of your time here with Mary."

"Are you sure?"

He nodded, waving her away.

A steward in a blue coat was in the passageway, carrying an armload of towels.

"Excuse me," Sarah said. "Where might I find steerage?"

She followed the steward's directions. Several feet from the portal leading to the steerage hold, Sarah noticed a foul odor getting stronger as she drew closer. Tending to Mrs. Carlton had required some unpleasantness no matter how clean she kept the lady, but Sarah was unprepared for the human suffering she beheld as she stepped through the door.

Bolted to the walls were about thirty canvas bunks, double-stacked. More than half of these were inhabited by men, women, or children, either asleep or softly moaning. Vomit dried on blankets and pillowcases, and the contents of an overturned bucket seeped under a bunk. A middle-aged woman went from bed to bed, wiping faces and giving sips of water. Rinsing out a mop in a pail was the young man who'd spoken to Sarah on deck.

Sarah covered her mouth with her hand, afraid she would add to the filth surrounding her. She was about to flee when the young man looked up at her and spoke.

"Well, hello, Miss Sarah. Are you lost?"

She shook her head slowly, taking shallow breaths. "I wanted to see what steerage was like. Those poor folks. It's dreadful down here!" After a pause, she added, "Is there anything I can do?"

"Can you stand the smell?"

"I think so."

The woman tending the people in the bunks looked over and gave Sarah a weary smile. "You should use your apron to tie up your dress a bit and keep it off the floor," she said, her voice a thick brogue. "And roll up your sleeves as well."

Hesitant to show her ankles, Sarah looked at the young man. With a grin, he turned his back and continued mopping. Sarah reached behind her back for her apron strings and hitched her dress up a couple inches.

"My whole family's taken with seasickness," said the woman, wiping the cheeks of a small boy. "And these two families—every one of them is sick. The ones that are well took their mats to the quarterdeck to get away from the smell."

"How long has it been since you've slept?" asked Sarah.

"Oh, I get bits and pieces here and there," said the woman. "Mr. David has been a blessin'. I don't know what we'd do—" She wiped the corner of her eye. "Excuse me. It's been a hard trip."

Sarah touched the woman's arm. "I can stay a little while. Why don't you take a nap?"

"Oh, I couldn't," protested the woman.

"Please let me help while I can," insisted Sarah, taking the bowl of wet cloths from the woman's hands.

After a few minutes, the woman's deep breathing could be heard from her bunk. "That was kind of you," said David, his mopping finished.

Sarah looked at the woman's tired face. *She's these children's mother,* Sarah thought. *I wish more people had been kind to my mother.*

I shouldn't be so happy to see her, David Adams thought when Sarah walked into the steerage compartment. It had been two days since the last time she'd helped out, and he'd found himself looking at the door every time someone walked in.

"I'm sorry I haven't been 'round lately," Sarah said. "Mrs. Carlton, my employer, is getting so weak that I'm afraid to leave her for long."

"Everything's in decent order now," David told her. "Why don't we sit on deck a while? I've been down here all day. Do you have time?"

"But I came to help."

The woman Sarah had helped before looked up from where she rested on her bunk. "Go on, children. Everyone's sleepin' now."

Outside the steerage compartment, David turned to Sarah. "Would you mind finding us a couple chairs while I change clothes?"

She smiled, and his weariness left him. "I'll try," she said.

Fairly racing down the passageway from his room, David came out on deck to find Sarah standing at the rail, the April trade winds moving her long hair about her shoulders. *Beautiful*, he thought, coming to an abrupt halt. He stared at her with his mouth agape until she sensed his presence and turned around.

"Oh," she said, her cheeks flushing. "I was admiring the water. I didn't expect you back so soon." She pointed to some deck chairs. "Will these be all right?"

"Of course," David said as they walked over to the chairs. "How long can you stay?"

"Not more than an hour," Sarah replied. "Mr. and Mrs. Carlton are resting, but I'll need to check on Mrs. Carlton."

"Are you her nurse?"

"Maid," she said quietly. "Where do you work?"

"My employer, Jacob Harvey, sent me to England to transact some business. I'm an accounting clerk with his investing firm in Charleston."

"What does one of those do?"

"One of—oh, you mean clerk. I keep books—ledgers of business transactions, prices and such—but I have other duties as well." *Like becoming engaged to Mr. Harvey's daughter*, he thought.

Taken by shyness, the girl studied her hands. David willed himself not to stare at her face. *She's apparently not well educated*, he thought, *but she has an intelligent face.* Her greatest charm was that she didn't seem to realize how intelligent and beautiful she was.

"May I ask you something?" he finally asked, aware that she would have to leave soon.

"Yes."

"The Carltons. Do they treat you well?"

She smiled. "Of course. Why do you ask?"

After a moment's hesitation, he went on. "There's a sadness about you."

A shadow crossed her face.

"I'm sorry," he said. "I'm prying. Please forgive me."

"Don't be sorry." she said. "You care about people, don't you?"

"I try to."

"You've spent most of your trip helpin' those people, yet you didn't have to. Why?"

"Please don't think more highly of me than you should," David said. "I've had to force myself to go through that steerage door every time."

"But you went."

"I put myself in their place. When Christ said, 'Do unto

others as you would have them do unto you,' He had people like them in mind."

"You're a Christian, then?"

"Yes," he answered, confused by the disappointment in her eyes. "Why do you look as though that's a bad thing?"

Sarah looked at him, her brown eyes serious. "The Nortons—a family I worked for once—said we servants should all be Christians, so Mr. Norton lined us up every Sunday mornin' and read Scripture to us. I didn't understand most of it or why he always appeared so angry at us as he read. Yet you are a Christian, and you are kind."

David had her hand in his before he realized he'd reached for it. "Sarah," he said earnestly. "I've met people who claimed to be Christians but didn't have an ounce of love in their hearts. To really become a Christian is to—"

"Excuse me, but are you Miss Brown?" A steward, clad in a red coat and black trousers, stood in front of them.

Sarah sat up, panic on her face. "Yes. Is something wrong with Mrs. Carlton?"

"I don't know, miss," said the steward. "But Mr. Carlton has requested that I find you."

She's gotten worse, and I was away, thought Sarah as she hurried to the Carltons' stateroom. Knocking softly, she pushed the door open. "I'm sorry I wasn't here," she said. "Has she gotten worse?"

"I didn't mean to frighten you," Mr. Carlton answered. "Mary would like to take a walk, and I need you to help me dress her."

"A walk?"

"Yes, dear." Opening her eyes, Mrs. Carlton smiled weakly from her pillow. "I feel a little better and would like to see something other than this closet of a room."

Mr. Carlton laughed. "I know what it is. You can smell land, Mary. The captain says we're only two days from shore."

"Two days." Mrs. Carlton sighed. "And I'm still alive, after all!"

"There it is—the United States!" said Mr. Carlton, pointing to a faint mass on the horizon. A cheer went up from the passengers, most of whom were lined against the port deck railing to catch the first sight of land.

My new life, Sarah thought. Her heart was filled with gratitude for her new employers and for what Miss Martin had done for her.

"Are you excited, child?" asked Mrs. Carlton from the deck chair her husband had pulled up to the rail.

"Yes, ma'am! I can't hardly take it all in!" On impulse, Sarah knelt and kissed Mrs. Carlton's hand. "Thank you, so much!"

"There, there girl," said the older woman. "You certainly made the return trip easier for Amos and me. We should be thanking you."

Blushing, Sarah rose to her feet. "I'll run down to our rooms and make sure we're packed up proper."

She was just outside the portal when she heard her name called. To her right was David, walking quickly in her direction. He was wearing a light gray coat and white drill trousers.

"David!" Sarah said, brightening. "I was afraid I wouldn't get to tell you goodbye."

David held out a package wrapped in brown paper. "I wanted to give you something." When Sarah held up a hand in protest, he pressed on. "It's a notebook I've been keeping for about a year. When I find a verse from the Bible that touches me, I write it down. I'd like you to have it."

Sarah was about to tell him that she couldn't read, when she realized that she would be ashamed for him to know that. Instead she said, "But you've spent a year writing in it, and now you're givin' it away?"

"I can start a new one. Please?"

"Thank you, David." Sarah turned the package over in her hand. "No one's ever given me a gift before."

"I've written the address of where I work in the inside cover. If you ever need help, you'll know where to find me."

A great lump formed in Sarah's throat. "Goodbye, David," she said, forcing a smile before going through the portal.

seven
1840-1841

"Really, Mary. How could you think of entertaining the Grimke sisters! You've had strange ideas before, but to have traitors in your own house!" Dorothy Bowman stirred her tea with vigor, the metal spoon clicking angrily against the sides of the cup. "Anyway, they've got no business coming back to visit. Let them stay up North where they belong!"

Mrs. Carlton took a sip from her cup. "There's no harm in listening. Besides, you know how I feel about slavery."

A frown creasing her attractive face, Mrs. Bowman shook her head. "People who haven't got Negroes should mind their own business. They eat rice, I'm sure. How are we supposed to operate a rice plantation without workers? I suppose those Grimkes asked you for money to print those awful little papers!"

"No, they didn't ask."

"But you gave them some, didn't you? Does Amos know you're throwing his money away like that?"

Sarah was standing just outside the parlor door with a silver tray of spiced cakes when Hannah, the cook, came up behind her. "Sarah, why haven't you taken the tray in yet?" she whispered.

"They're having a disagreement," Sarah whispered back. "I thought I should wait 'til they're finished."

"Finished? You wait for that, and you'll have cobwebs hanging from your earlobes. They're first cousins and talk that way all the time. Now, shoo!"

"Shoe?" Sarah looked down at her feet where the toes of her

brown morocco slippers peeked from under her skirt. "I've got them on."

Hannah sighed. "You Brits should learn to speak English. Take the tray in!" she said, giving Sarah a gentle push through the door.

Obediently, Sarah took the tray to a mahogany concertina table between the two women. "Fig cake, ma'am?" she asked Mrs. Carlton's visitor.

"Yes, I'll have one," said Mrs. Bowman, taking the flowered porcelain dish that Sarah handed her. "Mary, I suppose this is the maid you hired in England?"

Mrs. Carlton smiled from her Chippendale armchair. "In Bristol, right before we left." She gave Sarah a wink as she took a dish of cake from her hand. "Sarah has been a hard worker these three months."

Tapping at the front door sounded. The Carltons had no butler, so usually the servant who was closest to the front of the house answered it.

"I'll get that, ma'am," said Sarah, setting the cover to the butter dish on the tray. Mrs. Carlton's generous words sounded again in her mind as she made her way to the entrance hall. How different it was to be complimented for doing her best. Each word of praise from the Carltons made her work even harder.

Before pulling open the door, Sarah smoothed the gathers in her blue poplin dress, enjoying the crispness of the starched fabric. Mrs. Carlton didn't require her maids to wear caps, so Sarah kept her hair coiled loosely at the nape of her neck with a tortoise-shell comb she'd bought. It was nice to earn a salary decent enough to buy pretty things for herself.

"Good afternoon, sir," she said to the man on the front porch. About thirty years old, his tanned face was ruggedly handsome. Coal-black hair showed from beneath his hat. Brushing past her without a word, the man strode down the hall toward the parlor.

"Sir?" Sarah said, taking quick steps behind him.

"Ah, Mother," the man said, removing his hat as he entered the parlor. "My business in town is finished. Are you ready to leave?"

"Well, I suppose."

He bent down to put a kiss on Mrs. Carlton's cheek. "Mary, it's a pleasure to see you, as always. Is your health good?"

"It is, Jonathan. Will you stay and have some cake?"

"I'm afraid not," he said. "I've got some things to attend to before dark. Give my regards to Amos."

"He'll be disappointed that he missed you," said Mrs. Carlton.

"Yes, I can imagine." The man offered his arm to his mother and escorted her out of the house.

Hannah shopped for groceries every Tuesday and Saturday at the outdoor market near the fishing wharf. When Florence and Adele, the other maids, found out how eager Sarah was to accompany her, they gladly gave that responsibility to the English girl. They didn't enjoy carrying heavily loaded baskets in the July humidity.

Sarah wished the walk could be longer, for she was charmed by the beauty of Charleston. Middle Street was her favorite, lined with stuccoed houses whose hipped roofs were covered with pink or purple tiles. Wrought-iron garden gates, stair railings, and balconies abounded.

At the market while Hannah went from vendor to vendor, squeezing peaches, tapping melons, and smelling fish, Sarah was allowed to walk onto the Cooper River wharf. The salt air was invigorating, and she enjoyed watching the men laying traps for crabs. When the nets were pulled up, there were usually at least two or three blue crabs clinging to the bait. Turned inside out, the nets were then shaken roughly until the crabs gave up and dropped into a wooden half-barrel.

Almost as fascinating as the crabs were the gulls, screeching to each other overhead and sometimes trying to steal bait fish. Mingled with their cries was the slap of the water against barnacle-studded posts.

It was near this place, soon after she'd set ashore with the Carltons, that Sarah had first seen black people. Fascinated as she was by the darkness of their skin and hair, she tried not to stare at them. Staring was rude—Mother had taught her that long ago.

Sarah had been surprised to see several black people walking the streets without any chains. When she'd asked Hannah about it, the cook had explained that Negroes were allowed to run errands for their owners and to "hire out" on their own time. They weren't allowed on the streets of Charleston, however, between the night and morning drum beats unless they carried a pass from their owners.

"I think I'll make a peach cobbler for dessert tonight," Hannah was saying as they walked along the brick sidewalk leading from the market area, their arms loaded with purchases. "Mr. Carlton has a sweet tooth for cobbler."

"A sweet tooth," Sarah echoed, smiling.

"I suppose you never heard that one, either," said Hannah. "Well, he does."

"Have you been with them very long?"

"Years and years. I'd say fifteen. They're good folks to work for." Giving her a sideways glance, Hannah added, "They sure don't deserve the way Elizabeth treats them."

"Their daughter?"

Hannah's lips tightened. "You can call her that, but she doesn't act like a daughter should. Her portrait is hanging in the living room next to the fireplace."

"Doesn't she ever visit?" asked Sarah, who didn't recall seeing anyone come to call who resembled the lady in the portrait.

"Not for five years or so. It breaks their hearts to have an only child who's that spoiled and ungrateful."

Looking over her shoulder to make sure no one was walking behind them, Hannah continued. "Elizabeth got married eight years ago to a sorry, no-count of a man, Gerald Mobley. You should have seen the wedding. I baked the cake myself! Soon after they were married, Elizabeth asked Mr. Carlton to find her husband a position in his company."

A handsomely dressed young couple strolled by, and Sarah dropped back behind Hannah to make way for them on the sidewalk. When the couple had passed and was no longer in hearing range, Sarah stepped back in place next to Hannah.

"Elizabeth intended for Gerald to have an important position helping run the company. Mr. Carlton wasn't willing to demote Matthew Wesley, his assistant, who's been with him from the beginning. He offered Gerald a much lower position, saying he'd have to prove himself before getting more responsibilities.

"Elizabeth pouted and fumed but Mr. Carlton wouldn't change his mind, so Gerald took the job. Folks at the company began telling Mr. Carlton that Gerald was coming in late and sometimes didn't come in at all. When he did come to work, he told the other employees what to do, threatening to get them fired if they didn't cooperate."

Hannah shook her head. "After warning him time and time

again, Mr. Carlton had to let Gerald go."

Hannah and Sarah turned the corner onto palmetto-lined Dabney Street, where the Carltons' two-story brick house could be seen in the distance.

"Is that why they don't come to see the mister and missus?" asked Sarah.

The cook nodded. "After her husband was fired, Elizabeth came to the house in a screaming fit. Mr. Carlton wouldn't back down. He told her that he'd made Mr. Wesley a full partner, so if anything happened to him, Elizabeth and her husband couldn't get their hands on the business and ruin it. Elizabeth told her parents that she wouldn't set foot inside their house again. It broke their hearts, the dear old souls!"

Sarah's heart went out to the Carltons, who'd been so good to her. "It just ain't—I mean, isn't—right," she said to Hannah. "Here I am, still missing my mother, and she doesn't even visit hers!" The conversation ended as they entered the kitchen with their purchases.

"Tippecanoe!" Mr. Carlton snorted. "Mute as a mule is what he is! Why, I'll bet he hasn't a thought in his head that wasn't put there by his cronies!"

"Now, Amos," scolded his wife as she tied his wool scarf around his neck. "You're just trying to get out of going to Washington, and it won't work! I've never seen a presidential inauguration, and you gave me your word."

"You've never ridden a buffalo, either. I suppose the next thing you'll be wanting is to go out West."

"Who knows?" Standing on tiptoe, Mrs. Carlton kissed her husband's cheek. "Besides, you said yourself how good it'd be to see the Powells again. We'll have two weeks to catch up on old times!"

Sarah smiled in the next room as she fastened the catch on Mrs. Carlton's trunk. After almost a year of living with the couple, she was used to their affectionate bantering. *If I ever get married, I hope my husband is as good-natured as Mr. Carlton.* Suddenly, David came to her mind. *Does he think about me at all?* she wondered. He probably had more important things to occupy his thoughts. After all, she was just a servant.

Catching a peek at herself in Mrs. Carlton's mirror, Sarah tucked a stray wisp of chestnut-brown hair back into her comb. *Did he think I was pretty?* She'd looked wretched during the voyage, pale and thin after her years in Mrs. Gerty's employ. A year's time had made her figure more womanly, and her cheeks now glowed with health.

"Sarah, did you pack my blue wool shawl?" Mrs. Carlton was standing in the doorway to her room, her eyes on the trunk in the middle of the floor.

"No, ma'am," Sarah replied. "Remember, you told me I should put it in your canvas bag for the coach?"

Mrs. Carlton looked pleased. "What a sharp memory you have! Amos tells me that my cape will suffice, but I don't trust these March winds. They can still bring a bite to the cheeks."

"I hope the weather will hold for you and that you both have a wonderful time," Sarah added impulsively.

Stepping closer, Mrs. Carlton gave her a quick hug. "I think we shall."

Later that day, Sarah and Florence waved to the Carltons as the hired carriage pulled away from the house. They would be catching a coach to take them to Washington, D.C., for the festivities. The day after the inauguration of William H. Harrison, they would take a train on to Baltimore. Adele would spend the next three weeks in the country with her family, and Hannah would be staying with her sister in Charleston.

"We won't know what to do with ourselves!" Florence said after the carriage turned out of sight. "As long as we keep the house clean, Mrs. Carlton said we can do what we like."

"Don't forget we promised Mrs. Carlton we'd go to church every Sunday." The Carltons insisted that their servants attend worship services on the Lord's day. Hannah, who was Episcopalian, was always picked up in a carriage by some of her friends on their way to St. Philip's Church, while Adele, Florence, and Sarah rode with the Carltons to the Cathedral of Saint John and Saint Finbar on Broad Street.

Though she couldn't understand the language that was spoken during the service, Sarah knew it was about God. She'd questioned Mrs. Carlton about it, and the kindly lady had tried to explain God's love. That was harder to understand than the Latin, for Sarah certainly didn't feel lovable.

"Keep your heart open, Sarah. God will draw you to Him if you listen for Him," Mrs. Carlton had finally said.

David Adams was so intent on the papers before him that he did not hear the murmurs of greeting until Kathleen Harvey was standing in front of his desk.

"Goodness, David," said the comely young woman. "How your face scowls when you work!"

"Kathleen," said David, rising to his feet. "I apologize. I didn't know you were there."

She tugged at the wrist of one of her pale blue velvet gloves. "You haven't come by the house in almost a week, so I thought I should remind myself of what my fiancé looks like."

"I imagine I haven't changed that much." Startled by the sharpness of his voice, David smiled at her. "You look lovely.

Another new dress?"

Kathleen glanced down at the ecru muslin, with its shell buttons and blue silk underbodice. "Mother says I shall need at least a half-dozen more. You and I will be entertaining quite often, and people will want us to call on them as well."

"If it isn't my beautiful little girl!" A voice boomed out behind David. "And you came to visit your father at work. How flattering!"

"Oh, Papa!" With a giggle, Kathleen flounced around the desk and kissed the portly man on his cheek. "I can see you at home every day!"

Mr. Harvey feigned disappointment, shaking his head. "How soon they grow up!"

Giggling again, Kathleen covered her mouth with her hand. "You know why I'm here. I told you I was going to have David take me to lunch today!"

"Oh, yes. Now I remember." Turning to David, he put his hand on the young man's shoulder. "Take as long as you like, and here." Reaching into his pocket, he brought out a handful of bills and began to count some out.

"Mr. Harvey, I can't accept—" began David, mortified that the other employees in the office were watching them.

"Oh, don't be silly," said Kathleen, plucking the money from her father's hand. Adjusting the bow at the front of her Dunstable bonnet, she held out her arm. "Well, David?"

"Do you think we'll recognize Addison and Martha?" Amos Carlton stretched his legs as far as possible without hitting the man seated opposite him. The thirty-foot rear passenger car of the District of Columbia Railroad line was filled with people returning to Baltimore from the inauguration ceremony, and Amos, tired of people-watching, was in the mood to chat. "I suspect they look rather old after all these years."

Mary Carlton looked up from the book she was reading and smiled at her husband. "They may be wondering the same thing about us."

"Us? Why we look like schoolchildren next to our new president!"

"Amos, please don't talk about him so loudly. There may be someone around who voted for him," whispered Mary.

"Well, excuse me for being a bad sport about it, but I still don't see why Clay was passed over."

"You wouldn't have voted for him, either."

"True, but he would have had the integrity to run a real—"

Mary Carlton put her hand to her husband's lips. "Listen! Do you hear yelling?"

"Probably someone else who doesn't like the way Harrison—" He stopped suddenly, his head cocked. Over the drone of the wheels, he could hear frenzied voices from the front of the car shouting, "Axle's about to break! Stop the engine!"

"I believe I'll buy that pink gingham nightgown after all!" Florence came to an abrupt halt at the middle of Church Street, jerking Sarah's arm. "My aunt would love it for her birthday, and I still have time to send it to her."

"Are you sure this time?" asked Sarah, who'd been inside the corner apparel shop with her friend twice before that day.

"Very."

Sarah looked at Florence with affection. They'd had so much fun the past week, racing through their chores and taking long walks in Charleston. Sarah had told Florence about the time she'd spent on the ship with David, though she hadn't said anything about the notebook. That was her secret, and one day she'd learn how to read it.

"Do you want to see the statue before we go home?" asked Florence, once she'd finished her shopping. Tucking the parcel under her right arm, she linked her left arm through Sarah's. "It's at Washington Park, just one street over from where we are now."

"Who is he, and what happened to his arm?" asked Sarah when the bronze statue of a man in a flowing robe came into view.

"A Mr. William Pitt, from your neck of the woods."

"My neck of the woods?"

"Sorry. He was from England, like you. His arm, or rather the statue's arm, was lost when Charleston was fired at from the British in the war, so Mr. Carlton says."

Sarah was about to ask what the Englishman had done to endear himself to Americans, when she caught sight of a familiar face. There, some distance from them, was David! At his side with her hand in his was a lady, a fashionably dressed, attractive lady who motioned animatedly with her free hand as she talked.

"Let's go home," Sarah said to Florence, her cheeks burning as she turned away from the couple and headed in the opposite direction.

"But it's this way," said Florence.

Sarah didn't look to see in which direction her friend was pointing. "Please come with me. We can go that way later."

Hastening her steps, Florence caught up with Sarah. "What's wrong?" she said, panting slightly from the exertion.

"David."

"David? Where?"

"Don't look!" Sarah grabbed the girl's arm to keep her from

spinning around. "They'll see us!"

"They?"

"He has someone with him."

I was foolish to think about him so often! Sarah thought, propping herself up on her pillow. She'd gone to bed hours earlier, but thoughts of David drove sleep away.

The agony she'd felt all evening was unreasonable, she told herself. He'd been kind to her—just as he'd been kind to that woman in steerage—because he was a decent person. Nothing more.

Trying to fill her thoughts with other things didn't work. When sleep finally came, it was full of disjointed, hurried bits of dreams.

Sarah was frantically trying to scrub an oil stain from the carpet in Mrs. Gerty's library. To her horror, she'd poured the fluid out while cleaning a lamp-chimney, and the puddle grew larger, even as she sopped it up with rags. Somewhere in the house she could hear Mr. and Mrs. Gerty talking, their voices low and menacing She tried to call out to Ginny to ask for help with cleaning the rug, but her tongue was frozen and her mouth wouldn't form the words.

I'm only dreaming! Sarah realized, her eyes opening to sunlight slanting in from where the curtains met at her window. Confused, she could still hear the voices she'd heard in the dream. Then she realized that Florence was speaking with someone—a man—downstairs. Slipping out of bed, Sarah pulled her flannel robe over her nightgown and tied the sash. She was reaching for the comb on her dresser when she heard Florence cry out, "No! It can't be so!"

Sarah dashed from the room and down the stairs. In the front hall, a man was standing near the chair where Florence sat hunched over, her shoulders shaking. He looked up as Sarah descended the last steps.

"Mr. Wesley?" It had taken a moment for her to recognize Mr. Carlton's assistant, for his face was pale and drawn.

"I've brought bad news," he said. "Mr. and Mrs. Carlton were killed in a train wreck yesterday on their way to Baltimore."

Grabbing the banister rail, Sarah swallowed hard. "No!" The figure in front of her became blurred, but she could see that he was slowly nodding his head. "Oh, Mr. Wesley, how did it happen?"

"Believe me, it's best that you don't know all the details. I wish I didn't." He rubbed his forehead. "At least they didn't suffer. It was quick."

After Sarah had brewed some strong tea and persuaded Florence and Mr. Wesley to have some, they sat at the kitchen table.

"Do you have the addresses where Hannah and Adele are staying?" asked Mr. Wesley. "I'd rather send word to them than have them read about it in the newspaper."

"Yes," said Florence. "In the cupboard drawer. I'll get them for you."

Taking the piece of paper from the maid, Mr. Wesley looked at the two maids.

"There is something else you should know," he said. "I broke the news to Elizabeth—the Mobleys—before I came here. I don't know what her plans will be where all of you are concerned."

The next few days were busy. From the moment the coffins were delivered to the parlor until the funeral and burial at the Cathedral of Saint John and Saint Finbar, people came by to pay their respects. Having food prepared for the mourners was a constant duty, so Sarah, Adele, and Florence helped Hannah in the kitchen, speaking to each other in hushed tones.

After the burial, Elizabeth Mobley called the servants together in the living room. Sarah had been prepared to dislike the Carltons' ungrateful daughter, but she felt sorry for her. Elizabeth had sobbed throughout the funeral service, even trying to throw herself at the coffins as they were lowered into the ground.

"Humbug!" was what Hannah had whispered at the woman's emotional display, but it had brought fresh tears to Sarah's eyes.

"I want to thank you for serving my father and mother well," Elizabeth began, sitting on the sofa in front of them. "Unfortunately, I have no need of maintaining two houses, so I'm making arrangements to sell this one. You'll receive excellent references, but as of tomorrow morning, your services will no longer be required."

"Miss Elizabeth, I cooked for you when you were just a girl," protested Hannah. "You should have given us notice earlier so we could look for jobs. It isn't right to turn us out into the street!"

The woman sighed. "You can hardly blame me if my thoughts haven't been in order. I've barely slept these last four nights. Besides, you all have families, I'm sure, who can put you up until you find other employment."

"What about Sarah?" asked Florence. "She hasn't got any family."

"Then she's fortunate, isn't she?" sniffed Elizabeth. "She doesn't have relatives to turn their backs on her!"

"Can't you at least let her stay until she finds another job?" pressed Hannah. "She's too young to be on her own."

"Oh, all right!" answered Elizabeth, shrugging her shoulders. "I have a couple coming to look at the house Friday. It would be better to keep it aired out and the furniture dusted. You may stay here until Thursday afternoon if you'll do those chores." She narrowed her eyes at Sarah. "You must be out by Thursday afternoon, do you understand? And if I discover anything missing, I'll alert the sheriff at once."

eight
1841

The *Charleston Courier* contained advertisements placed by homeowners looking for servants, Hannah had told Sarah before she'd left. After a sleepless night, Sarah decided she would walk to the stone building that housed the Charleston Library Society and ask the librarian to read the newspaper advertisements to her.

Stepping to the mirror above her dresser, Sarah peered at the dark circles under her eyes. *No one will want to hire me. I look beastly from tossing and turning all night,* she thought, frowning at her reflection. At least the green linen dress she was wearing brought out the rich hues in her chestnut hair. She would need to trim it soon, she thought as she reached for her comb. It was down to her waist, and when she coiled it into a bun, it pulled heavily against the back of her head.

Mrs. Carlton's gray hair had been even longer than Sarah's, though not nearly as thick. Adele and Sarah had combed Mrs. Carlton's hair every night and braided it in the mornings, for the woman's slight rheumatism prevented her from doing it herself.

The thought of Mrs. Carlton made Sarah's eyes burn. *You mustn't cry now,* she scolded herself. *It won't bring them back, and you've got to look presentable to find work.*

An abrupt silence made her realize someone had been knocking at the front door. *Oh dear, it's Mrs. Mobley. She'll kick me out for ignorin' her,* Sarah thought, dropping her comb to the floor.

Halfway down the stairs she realized she was still in her

74

stocking feet, but it was too late to go back for shoes. Hastening through the hallway, she threw open the front door.

Elizabeth Mobley was nowhere in sight, but a man was walking toward a carriage parked in the street. At the sound of the door, the man turned around.

"Mr. Bowman," said Sarah. She'd only seen Jonathan Bowman twice before: the day that his mother had come to call and at the Carltons' funeral. Neither time had he spoken to Sarah, so she was startled when he removed his hat and took a step toward her.

"So, Elizabeth has a heart after all. I didn't expect anyone to be here. Rumor is that she's kicked out the servants." His tanned face crinkled when he smiled, and his blue eyes shone under a fringe of dark eyelashes.

"She very kindly said I could stay till Thursday while I look for another situation."

"Oh, she's the soul of kindness. A saint." He started walking toward the door. "Anyway, I'm glad someone was here. There's something I have to get."

He was only a few feet away when Sarah gathered up the nerve to protest. "I'm sorry, sir, but you mustn't take anything from the house."

"I mustn't?" he said, his faint drawl vanishing as he clipped his words to imitate her accent. He sidestepped her and entered the house.

"Mr. Bowman, you must leave this house at once," Sarah said, trying to keep her voice steady as she trailed him through the hall and up the stairs.

Ignoring her, he stepped onto the second-floor landing and made his way to the closed door of the Carltons' bedroom. His hand was on the knob when he turned back to look at her.

Sarah froze. *What am I doing, following him into* . . . Biting her lower lip, she wondered what to do. Run outside and cry for help?

The sound of drawers being pulled open turned Sarah's fear into anger. How dare he try to take something! She ran into the Carltons' room. "Sir, you've no right to mess up this room. Have you no respect for the dead?"

Pushing in the bottom drawer of the carved fruitwood dresser, Jonathan Bowman moved to a black lacquered chest against the opposite wall.

"Perhaps you can help. Have you seen a handkerchief with some yellow birds embroidered around it?" He was rifling through the contents of the top drawer.

Surely she hadn't heard him right. "A handkerchief?"

"Yes," he said, not looking up. "My mother made it for Mary when they were little girls. Look. Here it is!" He brought out a yellowed square of linen, with childish, uneven stitching around the edges.

"You can't take that from here," Sarah said, stepping back to the doorway and blocking his passage.

"Oh?" He was coming toward her, his eyebrows raised. "And I suppose you're going to forbid me to leave this room?"

Hands trembling, Sarah nodded, hoping her face didn't betray her fear.

The corners of his mouth turned up again. "Well, if I'm stuck here, I might as well have a nap."

Before she could blink her eyes, he was sitting on the edge of the bed, pulling off a leather boot.

"What—"

"You know, I was up all hours last night. I figured I'd try to squeeze in a rest today after I ran this little errand for Mother." Dropping the boot to the floor, he began tugging at the other one.

"Anyway, this is better. I've got a lovely young maiden to watch over me and see that I sleep undisturbed."

When his fingers started unfastening the top button of his dark blue shirt, Sarah covered her eyes with her hand. "Sir, you aren't going to undress in here, are you?"

He sounded surprised. "Why, of course. You don't expect me to sleep fully clothed, do you?"

"All right. I'm leaving," she said, her shoulders falling. "Only, please wait and ask Mrs. Mobley about the handkerchief. I don't want to be arrested!"

"Arrested? That's ridiculous. It's just a handkerchief."

"But Mrs. Mobley said she'd tell the sheriff if anything turned up missing after I leave."

His laugh made her flinch. "That's what all this fuss is about? Prison? By the way, you can look now. My shirt's fastened again." He reached down for one of his boots. "We don't put girls in prison for missing hankies. I suppose the English send them to the gallows?"

Shaking her head, Sarah thought, *Why doesn't he just leave?*

His boots back on his feet, Jonathan Bowman stood up and stepped toward Sarah. "My mother made this handkerchief for Mary when they were children. Even though they grew apart, they were very close at one time. I'll leave a note downstairs for Elizabeth if you're going to have nightmares about prison cells."

"Thank you," Sarah whispered, backing out of the doorway. The ordeal had strained her raw nerves, and to her embarrassment, tears flowed.

"You're quite a cry-baby, aren't you?" the unwelcome visitor asked. "You'd probably be halfway decent to look at if you weren't so weepy-eyed." After walking through the doorway, he stopped in front of her, slowly reached out a hand, and touched a curl of brown hair at her shoulder. "I'll wait in the carriage while you pack your things."

Her tears dried up and her head snapped back. "Mr. Bowman, you have misunderstood what kind of person I am!"

"Misunderstood?"

"Yes, very much!" she said, spitting out the words.

"I don't understand." He scratched his head. "Didn't you say that you're looking for a job?"

"As a domestic, Mr. Bowman—nothing more."

Shrugging his shoulders, he brushed a piece of lint from his cuff. "Of course. Whatever did you think I meant? My mother could use a maid, and I'm prepared to hire you if you want the job."

"A maid?"

"That's what you are, right?"

"I'm sorry," she said, feeling foolish for jumping to conclusions. Just then, Sarah remembered something from a conversation between Mrs. Bowman and Mrs. Carlton.

"You have slaves, don't you?" she asked.

"Yes, some," he said. "But Mother's getting difficult, and she doesn't trust the Negroes anymore. I'm at my wit's end as to how to handle her."

"Well, I had hoped to stay here in Charleston—"

"Perfect! In two months, Mother will be coming back here to live in our town house. She leaves the plantation every year from early May until first frost. There's danger of malaria during the warm months."

"Don't the slaves get malaria?"

"Not very often. The Negroes seem to have some natural immunity, perhaps from the African climate. I don't get sick either, so I won't be staying here in town with Mother, if that makes you feel better."

Crossing his arms, he impatiently drummed his fingers on his sleeve. "Of course, if you're not interested, I'm sure we'll have no trouble finding someone else."

Sarah knew she had to make up her mind quickly. *My savings can't last forever, and it might take some time to find a position from the newspaper,* she thought. *I won't have to be around Mr. Bowman very much.*

"Thank you," she finally said. "I'll pack right away."

In front of the Carltons' house, Jonathan inhaled deeply of his cigar. Squinting his eyes, he looked at the second-floor window where the girl was hurriedly gathering her things. *She's a real beauty,* he thought. He flicked the ashes from his cigar into the street. *They're so easily fooled when they want to be!*

"My grandfather, Pierce Bowman, built Magnolia Bend between 1760 and 1770." Jonathan pointed toward the river. "I'm glad he picked the Ashley River to build on. It's not the best river for growing rice, but it's the closest to Charleston. Shipping's easier."

Sarah nodded from across him in the carriage. They'd been on the road for two hours, and she was beginning to have misgivings. She didn't expect Mrs. Bowman to be as kind as Mrs. Carlton, especially after what her son had said about her being "difficult."

Get hold of yourself! Sarah reproached herself. *You're not a thirteen-year-old child.* She could be satisfied, she told herself, as long as she wasn't mistreated. *It's good that I'm returning to Charleston with Mrs. Bowman in a few weeks,* she thought. *If things are intolerable, I can look for another job.*

The horses slowed as the road inclined sharply for two-hundred feet. Then, turning to the right, the carriage entered a shadowy avenue lined with towering oaks. High limbs stretched across the lane and met to form a high, sun-dappled ceiling.

The horses picked up speed again, hungry for their oats. At the end of the avenue waited an imposing two-story white house. Its many-windowed front was interrupted by huge white columns and delicate wrought iron.

"What do you think?" asked Jonathan.

"Your home is lovely, sir," said Sarah, thinking privately how little the appearance of a house had to do with how the people living within it treated each other.

Veering to the left around the house was a curved road. It ran through a garden to a side door. The carriage halted several feet away, and Mr. Bowman was greeted respectfully by eight dark-skinned servants.

"Miz Dora, she be lying down," said a stooped man with white hair.

"I suppose she still has a headache?"

The old man nodded. "Yassir."

Jonathan sighed as he helped Sarah alight from the carriage. "All right. Violet, show Miss Sarah to her room—the corner bedchamber next to my mother's. Then find her something to eat." He turned to a much younger black man. "Anson, saddle my horse and bring her here. I want to look at the trenches before it gets dark."

"Is there anything I should be doing?" Sarah asked.

"No, not today. Violet can show you around if you wish." Turning, he followed Anson toward the stables.

A girl about her own age stepped forward, and Sarah assumed she was Violet. The slave girl directed two adolescent boys to carry Sarah's small trunk, and she led Sarah up a short flight of stone steps and through the door. The first room they entered was a parlor, spacious and airy. A wide passageway was next with a mahogany-railed staircase curving toward them.

At the top of the stairs, Violet put a brown finger to her lips. "We have to be quiet, Missy. Miz Dora." She pointed to a paneled door.

Following the girl through an open door at the end of the upstairs hall, Sarah moved aside so the boys could set the trunk on the floor next to a four-poster bed.

When the boys had left, Violet closed the door softly, walked over to the trunk, and knelt down to open the latch.

Confused, Sarah watched Violet. She'd always packed and unpacked for herself, as was expected of servants. Could this girl be thinking she was a guest or relative?

"Violet?" she said as the girl swung the lid open.

The girl turned her head to look at her. "Yes, Missy?"

"Why are you unpacking my things?"

"Why?" Violet looked as confused as Sarah. "If I don't put them on pegs, they'll get wrinkled." Turning her attention back to the trunk, she scooped up Sarah's favorite dress, a dark-blue calico.

"But. . ." Following Violet to a wide chifforobe next to the fireplace, Sarah watched her fluff out the folds of the dress. "I can do that," she finally said.

Violet smiled agreeably, but didn't stop smoothing the blue fabric with her hands. After she put the dress away, she started back to the trunk.

"Wait." Sarah reached out and touched the girl's arm. "You're not supposed to unpack my clothes."

Something akin to fear came into Violet's brown eyes.

"What do you mean, miss?"

"I'm a maid here. Mr. Bowman hired me this morning."

The slave girl shifted uneasily from one foot to the other.

"Do you understand?" asked Sarah.

The girl shook her head. "You're white," she whispered.

"You've never seen a white servant?"

"No, missy," she said, and reached down for another dress.

Violet was determined not to stop, so Sarah figured she'd at least help with the three remaining dresses and her other belongings. Silently they worked, side by side, while once in a while Violet darted a quick glance at the white girl.

When they'd finished unpacking, Violet led Sarah down the stairs, through the dining room and pantry, to another door. It was still daylight when they stepped outside, though an evening chill was settling in. They walked over a short path leading to a brick building.

"Missy Sarah, this is Leah. She's the cook," Violet said as they entered the kitchen. To Leah, she asked, "Do you have anything ready to eat?"

The older black woman, her head wrapped in a brightly colored square of fabric, looked up from the biscuits she was rolling. She looked at Sarah as if surprised to see a white woman in her kitchen.

"Suppah ain't ready for a while, but I got some sweet potato bread and a piece o' ham."

"That sounds good. I haven't eaten all day," said Sarah to the woman. She saw the cook's shoulders relax. "May I eat in here?"

Violet's eyebrows shot up. "In the kitchen?"

"I've spent most of my life in kitchens," Sarah said, taking the pewter dish that another woman—her hair also bound up in a scarf—handed her.

Though Violet sat at the huge planked oak table with Sarah, she would not eat. Sarah chewed slowly to keep from wolfing down the food. It was delicious, and not just because she was ravenous. The sweetness of the bread went well with the salty ham.

The kitchen, with its brick floor and whitewashed walls, was as long as the Carltons' whole house. The ceiling was smoked almost black. A wide fireplace took up most of one wall, and stirring the contents of a big iron pot hanging over the fire was another slave woman. A boy sat on a low stool, slowly turning the handle of a spit on which at least a half-dozen hens were roasting.

When Sarah finished eating, Violet asked if she'd like to see the rest of the plantation. Thanking Leah for the meal, Sarah walked with Violet outside around another path of flat rocks. It led to a dirt lane and several small wooden buildings.

"That's the smokehouse," said Violet, pointing to the first building. "Those two houses are the sundry barns, and the mill's on the other side."

Though Sarah paid close attention to what Violet said, she was more interested in the girl herself. "How long have you lived here?" she asked, hoping Violet wouldn't think her too nosy.

"Three years."

"Where did you live before here?"

"Master Lucas's house, down the river a bit. He sold some of us to Master Bowman."

"Are you treated well here?"

Violet locked eyes with Sarah, gave a quick, solemn nod, then pointed to another cabin. "Over there is the grain house."

Back upstairs in her room, Sarah was cleaning her hands at the washstand when a knock sounded at the door. Standing in the hallway was a black woman whom she hadn't seen earlier. "Miz Dora want to see you now."

Mrs. Bowman looked up as Sarah walked into the room. "Pull a chair up to the bed so we can talk."

Quickly, Sarah obeyed. Mrs. Bowman seemed to have lost weight. The flesh around her chin sagged loosely, and the complexion Sarah remembered as being lovely was now milky pale.

"Do you remember me?" asked Mrs. Bowman.

"Yes, ma'am. You came to see Mrs. Carlton last year."

"I look quite different now, don't I?" said Mrs. Bowman, her lower lip trembling slightly. "You've gotten prettier, and I've turned into an ugly old hag."

"Oh no, ma'am. That's not so!" protested Sarah.

"I despise a liar," said the woman sharply. "Are you trying to flatter me?"

Sarah took a deep breath. *You can always look for another job in just a few weeks,* she told herself. "Mrs. Bowman, you don't look like a hag. But if it's honesty you want, you look like you've been ill. Is that why you couldn't come to the funeral?"

"Yes." Mrs. Bowman's lip started trembling. "I wanted to go, but my head hurt so badly that I couldn't tolerate the drive. You think Mary and Amos would have understood?"

Mrs. Bowman had such childlike longing in her expression, that Sarah felt compassion. "They were kind," she said. "They wouldn't have wanted you to travel when you were ill."

"That's right," Mrs. Bowman said, almost eagerly. "But I made sure that Jonathan went, even though I was afraid to be here without him. I was in terrible pain."

"Is there anything I can do for you? Does your head still hurt?" asked Sarah.

"It hurts almost constantly, but I feel a little better now that my son is home. I've been asking him to hire a white girl to help me, but he said it wasn't necessary. I was so pleased when he told me about you."

"Pleased, ma'am?"

"Oh, yes! Mary had good sense when it came to picking dependable servants." She sniffed faintly. "She had good sense about other things too—more than I gave her credit for at the time."

Not fully understanding what response was expected of her, Sarah nodded. "Yes, ma'am."

Suddenly, the woman slipped a hand out from under the sheet and grabbed Sarah's. "I feel that I can trust you, especially if Mary trusted you." She lowered her voice. "I need to hear it from you, though. Can you keep a secret?"

Sarah blinked, startled. "I can."

"Have you ever kept an important secret?"

After a moment, Sarah answered. "Yes, ma'am." *Oh, Mother,* she thought. *I wanted to run into your arms and tell you how mean Mrs. Gerty was, but I pretended to be happy for your sake.* "A very important one."

"Good!" Letting go of Sarah's hand, Mrs. Bowman leaned forward. "Tiptoe over to the door and see if anyone's listening," she whispered.

"Listening?"

"Outside the door. Hurry!"

Rising, Sarah slipped to the door, turned the knob, and pulled it toward her a little, peeking out the narrow crack.

"Not like that! Throw it open quickly!" said the woman from the bed.

The door made a loud "whuff" as Sarah pulled it open. Sticking her head into the upstairs hall, she looked both ways.

"No one's there, ma'am," she said, closing the door again.

"We still have to talk softly," Mrs. Bowman said, motioning for Sarah to sit. "The slaves are planning to revolt soon. I fear they want to kill Jonathan and me and take over Magnolia Bend. That's why I get so many headaches lately." She closed her eyes for a second. "They're poisoning my food a little bit at a time."

When Sarah didn't respond, the woman grew agitated. "You're looking at me like Jonathan does—as if I'd lost my mind. I tell you, it's true!"

"Ma'am, I didn't mean to look at you like that," said Sarah. "It's just the Negro servants seem nice."

"So, you've met them all?"

"Not all of them, I'm sure. But Violet and Leah and those that I've met—"

"We have over one hundred eighty Negroes," interrupted Mrs. Bowman. "Would it be ridiculous to think that some of them are unhappy enough to want to kill us?" She shook her head. "We've treated them almost like family. We've even made sure that each cabin has a full bolt of mosquito netting for the beds. Most planters wouldn't bother with that expense. But, you know, the longer I live, the more I realize that the people you do the most for are sometimes the most ungrateful!"

Sarah didn't know what to think. Mrs. Bowman surely knew more than she did about her own slaves. She remembered how badly she had felt when Mrs. Gerty had held her wages back. To work for nothing, year after year—perhaps Mrs. Bowman was right.

"Has Mr. Bowman been getting headaches?" Sarah asked.

"No, but I'm worried about him. You see, they won't try to kill us the same way. It would look too suspicious."

"Have you told Mr. Bowman?"

A look of pain washed across the woman's face. "Jonathan won't listen. He thinks I'm imagining things. I'm not imagining the looks they give each other when they think we're not watching!"

Suddenly, the older woman's face brightened. "Now that you're here, we can do something about it. I've been making plans."

Sarah swallowed hard before asking, "Plans?"

"Yes. I've sent word to Leah that I want all my meals sent up here, and yours, too—on account of my headaches, you see." Her voice took on a conspiratorial tone. "We'll switch trays as soon as Ben and Lucy leave the room. If you start getting headaches, we'll know they've been plotting against me.

"But don't worry," she added hastily. "As soon as your headaches come—if they do—we'll have the evidence, and you can stop. I wouldn't let you eat enough to kill yourself."

That didn't make Sarah feel any better. "Why wouldn't they poison my tray along with yours?"

Mrs. Bowman smiled. "I wondered that, myself, but after thinking it over, I know they wouldn't. If we both got sick, it would prove that they're poisoning the food."

Folding her arms together across her chest, Mrs. Bowman looked pleased with herself. "You have to outthink them, just like playing chess."

nine
1841

"Sir, may I talk with you?"

Jonathan Bowman looked up, folded his newspaper, and placed it on the settee next to him. "Come in."

"I'd best shut the door, if you don't mind," said Sarah, still standing in the doorway of the library.

"By all means. I've been expecting you."

Expecting me? Sarah wondered. *Why?* Closing the door, she took a couple steps forward. "Sir, it's about—"

"Why don't you sit down."

Slipping into a gold damask chair across from Mr. Bowman's settee, Sarah took a deep breath. "It's about the job. I've reconsidered and can't accept it." She hurried on. "I know it's a long ride back to Charleston, but I can pay someone to take me in the morning."

Jonathan studied Sarah's face with his midnight-blue eyes. Clasping his hands behind his head, he leaned against the high back of the sofa. "I take it that you've talked with Mother," he said, a trace of a smile on his face.

"I have, and I can't accept the terms of my employment."

"She wants you to stand at her door with a gun, eh?"

"No, sir. Mrs. Bowman plans to have me switch meals with her to test for poison."

Jonathan sighed. "She's obsessed with this conspiracy idea. Did she tell you she kept a pistol under her pillow while I was in Charleston?"

"Perhaps there's some truth to what she fears," said Sarah.

Jonathan shook his head. "Not here. Believe me. I keep a

close eye on my people." He leaned forward, his arms propping his weight on his knees. "It's that abolitionist tract we found last October! I wish she'd never found out about it!"

"Excuse me, sir?"

"There's a seditious little pamphlet printed by a freed slave in Boston called the Appeal. It tries to stir up the Negroes to overthrow their masters. I have it right here," he said, rising and walking over to a roll-top desk. From the bottom drawer he brought out a thin booklet with worn edges, about the size of his palm. "Would you like to see it?"

Sarah looked down at her hands. "I can't read."

Shrugging his shoulders, Jonathan sat back down. "I'll read some of it to you, then, and you'll understand my mother's fears." Opening the pamphlet, he began to read:

> *If you commence, make sure work—do not trifle, for they will not trifle with you—they want us for their slaves and think nothing of murdering us in order to subject us to that wretched condition—therefore, if there is an attempt made by us, kill or be killed.*

He slapped the booklet shut. "A white steward on a brig from Boston thought he would hand some of these out to our Negroes in Charleston while his ship was in dock. A loyal slave showed one to his master, and the steward was arrested and put in prison for a year. That was a few years ago, and I didn't think any of my people ever saw this piece of trash—until we found this in one of the quarters." Shaking his head, Jonathan frowned. "One of my most trusted workers. I used to send him to Charleston on errands by himself."

"What happened to him?" asked Sarah.

"He's dead."

"For having that paper?"

Fixing his eyes steadily on hers, Jonathan replied, "The penalty for trying to lead a revolt is hanging. That's the law in South Carolina. He knew better than to have something like that in his possession."

Still horrified, Sarah asked, "Do you kill them when they displease you?"

"Of course not!" Jonathan looked at Sarah as if she'd lost her mind. "What kind of businessman would I be if I mistreated my laborers!"

When she didn't answer, he went on. "The Negroes here are well fed, clothed, and taken care of. There are inequalities all over the world, Sarah. Take your England, for example. I've heard there are children as young as six years old working in the factories and mines. I don't send them out in the rice fields that young. When you've lived here longer, you'll understand the way things are. Now, let's talk about Mother."

"She wants me to switch meals with her to test for poison." Sarah shook her head. "I can't do that."

"Sarah," he said, smiling at her as if she were a child. "Do you think the servants would poison an old woman?"

Sarah pondered his question. "No, perhaps not. But she's asking me to risk my life."

"And your life is of great value to you, I assume."

It wasn't the words so much as the faint smirk at the corner of his mouth that enraged her. "Mr. Bowman, it's true that I'm just a servant, but my life is my own!"

"You're right, of course." He held both hands up in front of him, placatingly. "I didn't mean to say that." Putting his hands down again, he lowered his voice. "I just wanted to see the fire in those dark eyes again."

"Sir?" Not sure if she'd heard him right, Sarah wondered

whether to leave the room.

"Nothing," he said. "Please reconsider staying with my mother. I can't leave my work to calm her fears all the time. You'd have no work to do other than keeping her company."

"But the food?"

"I know it sounds crazy, but it would reassure her if you could prove that she's wrong. Perhaps then she'll stop imagining plots." Suddenly, he sat up straight. "I've got it! You save half the food on your tray for me, and I'll have it when Mother's asleep."

Sarah gave a small sigh. "You're that sure there's no poison?"

"That sure."

"Then I'll try it myself—as long as my head doesn't hurt."

"Thank you, Sarah," he said, rising to open the door for her. "My mother can be quite pleasant when she's not worrying. You may even feel at home here, one day."

"My husband, Charles, used to tell me all the time, 'Dorothy, holding your hand is like touching the cream at the top of the milk bucket!'" Mrs. Bowman held both hands out for Sarah to see. "I've always kept a little mineral oil spread on them at night, and I use the smallest amount of soap when washing my hands."

"Your hands are lovely, ma'am."

The woman's eyes drifted to the tray on Sarah's lap. "Is the food suitable?"

"It's delicious," answered Sarah, breaking a hot-buttered biscuit in half. "What do you call this?" She pointed to the chunks of seafood and vegetables in a brown, gravylike liquid served over rice.

"It's gumbo. We had it at the Jordans' house. Their cook is

a Creole from New Orleans, so I asked Caroline Jordan to let Leah go over and learn how to cook it." Mrs. Bowman spooned down her own gumbo with relish. "I don't believe it's ever tasted quite so good," she said.

Later that night, Sarah lay in bed wondering if her head would start hurting. *I don't believe I've been poisoned,* she thought. *And Mrs. Bowman seems to like me.* Perhaps she had made the right decision, but what would David think of her working for people with slaves? She didn't think he'd approve.

Sarah wished she could talk with David about many things. Perhaps he could explain the ache she had for something she couldn't recognize, much less understand. *There's something out there that I need so much, but I don't know what it is,* she thought.

She had her eyes half open when the doorknob turned slowly. As the door drifted open, Sarah sat up in time to see a dark form slip inside the room.

"Oh, missy. I'm sorry to wake you up!" said a voice.

"Violet?"

"Yes, miss. It's me all right." In the dimness, Sarah could see the girl carried a bundle.

"I've got a log. I thought I'd make a little fire to break the chill in the room," Violet said, walking over to the fireplace.

Sarah didn't know what to say, so she watched the girl spread kindling in the hearth. From a bucket she carried, Violet poured a glowing ember on the kindling, picking up the poker to stir the wood. "When that burns a little, I'll put the log on top," she said.

Finding her tongue, Sarah smiled. "Thank you. The fire will be nice. If you'll tell me where to find the wood, I'll lay my own and save you the trouble."

Hesitating, Violet walked toward the bed. "Miss Sarah," she said meekly, "we been told what to do. If you do our work, then we'll be in trouble."

Watching Violet wring her hands, Sarah's heart went out to the girl. "I don't want to get you in trouble, but I'm not used to being waited on." Then, a thought dawned upon her. "Am I causing a problem?"

Violet smiled. "Not if you let us do our work."

"As you can see, this home has been well cared for," said Elizabeth Mobley, walking over to touch the east wall of the sitting room. "The wallpaper came from France just last year, and the paneling was polished every week."

Kathleen Harvey nudged her fiancé beside her on the sofa. "The wallpaper has to go," she said under her breath. "Roses are so outdated!" To Elizabeth, she smiled sweetly. "Have you thought about our offer?"

Taking her chair opposite the couple, Elizabeth cleared her throat. "I understand why a young couple just starting out would want a good price. It's a lot lower than what I asked, though."

Kathleen's face fell. "Oh, dear. I had nightmares that this would happen!" Clasping her hands tightly in her lap, she gave Elizabeth a trembling smile. "We can't afford to go any higher."

"Not even to halve the difference?"

Kathleen shook her head regretfully. "It's very kind of you to offer, and I wish our circumstances would permit. I suppose it wasn't meant to be."

The man sitting beside her looked startled. "Wait a minute," he began. "We decided that—"

Raising her voice, Kathleen drowned out her fiancé. "We'll

have to take that little house on Charlotte Street." Rising, she motioned for the man to follow. "Come, David. We won't take any more of Mrs. Mobley's time."

The young man was halfway to his feet when Elizabeth held up her hands in protest. "Please stay. It's possible that we can work this out."

As the couple sat back down, Kathleen's eyebrows raised expectantly. "Yes?"

Giving a heavy sigh, Elizabeth nodded her head. "I need to settle my parents' estate as soon as possible. My husband needs the capital to invest in a business venture. My parents died last week, you know."

"I'm sorry," offered David. He couldn't remember seeing a death notice in the newspaper for any Mobleys. "Were they ill?"

"Oh, no!" she said. "Didn't you hear about the train wreck near Baltimore last week? My mother and father were killed in that wreck."

He'd only read about one couple from Charleston who'd died on that train, a businessman and his wife. *Of course!* he thought. *Their last name wouldn't be Mobley.* "Your father is—was he Amos Carlton?"

"Yes." Reaching for a handkerchief, Elizabeth blew her nose loudly. "They were the finest people. Everyone loved them."

"The Carltons." David spoke as if in a daze. "What happened to their servants?"

Elizabeth looked puzzled. "Oh," she finally said. "You'll need servants. I'm sure the ones who worked here have found other employers."

"Do you know which employers?"

"No, I'm afraid I don't," said Elizabeth. Then she remembered the note that Jonathan had left her, telling that the English maid was in his employ. *Doesn't matter,* she told herself. *I'm here to sell a house, not to help this greedy couple find servants.*

"Perhaps we shouldn't buy the house after all," said Kathleen, elbowing her fiancé while lowering her eyelashes at Elizabeth. "You must have so many memories. . . ."

"Well, yes, but my husband needs the money. Only, he was hoping to get a little more than—" Suddenly, she sat up straight. "I tell you what. I'll take my carriage home now. He's there resting. I'll ask him if he can live with your offer, and come right back and let you know. You can stay here and look around some more."

"Thank you so much!" said Kathleen, jumping up from her seat. "I'm so thrilled, and look at my fiancé. He's speechless!"

Sarah lived in this house, thought David. *She never contacted me. I wonder where she is now?* He let his hand rest reverently on the carved cherry of the sofa arm. *She probably dusted this chair.* For the hundredth time, David reminded himself that he'd only known the girl briefly. *She's forgotten me,* he thought. *Why can't I get her out of my mind?*

When Elizabeth had left, Kathleen turned angrily to David. "You almost ruined everything. We're getting this beautiful house for a steal!"

David looked up. "We're not going to take advantage of the lady, Kathleen. She just lost her parents, and she might not be thinking rationally."

"Oh, nonsense! You heard her say it's been a week." Turning on her heel, Kathleen studied the wall. "I believe a fleur-de-lis pattern would make this room look more modern, don't you?"

David watched her go about the room, examining the

furnishings. *Why did I let myself get pressured into this?*

He winced as Kathleen squealed. "These curtains are brand new—no fade lines!"

I don't even like her very much. Overwhelmed by thoughts of living with Kathleen for the rest of his life, David groaned.

"Oh, don't be so grumpy!" Kathleen said over her shoulder as she turned up the lining of the curtains on the next window. "We can buy new ones if you don't like these."

David put his head in his hands. "It's no use, Kathleen," he said. "I can't."

"Can't what?" she said, walking over to stand in front of him. "Are you ill?"

"No," he said bleakly. "I can't get married."

Kathleen laughed. "Of course you can, you silly thing!"

David knew that he'd never get another chance. "Please sit down," he said, looking up at her.

"David, you're serious, aren't you?" Taking her place next to him, Kathleen put a hand on his arm. "Is it because of the way I got that woman to lower the price?"

She took his silence for agreement. "That's business, dear. I learned that from my father, and look where he is today."

"Kathleen, please listen!" David said, turning to her. "I've not been honest with you or with myself. It's killing me to have to hurt you, but I don't want to get married."

"You have last-minute jitters, that's all," she said reassuringly. "We still have two months for you to calm down." Her face brightened suddenly. "I know! You've been working so hard, Papa says. Perhaps you need a rest from your job for a few days. I'll ask Papa to let you—"

"No!" David interrupted. "That's why I can't marry you. You and 'Papa' would run our lives! I'd be a houseboy for you to order around, and you'd run to your father when I didn't obey."

"David, I can't believe you're saying such mean things!" Kathleen said. Covering her face with her hands, she burst into tears.

David almost changed his mind. Kathleen's tears were nothing new to him, but this time she was truly in pain. *It wouldn't be fair to her,* he thought. *She should marry a man who will love her.*

"Kathleen, if I could do anything to undo the hurt I've caused you—"

"You can marry me!" she sobbed. "What will everyone say? You're practically leaving me at the altar!"

Pulling a handkerchief from his waistcoat pocket, David tried to wipe her face. "Oh, give me that!" she commanded, dabbing at her eyes.

The grandfather clock marked off the seconds against the wall behind them. When Kathleen turned to David, her green eyes were filled with sadness. "You don't love me?"

He shook his head. "I'm sorry—not enough to get married."

"Well, I like that!" she said, jumping to her feet. "You can explain to Mrs. Mobley when she returns. I'm going to see what Papa has to say about this!"

Before disappearing through the door, Kathleen threw one parting shot. "And you're such a fine Christian, everybody says! What would they say if they could hear you now?"

The walls shuddered with the splintering slam of the door. Leaning his head on his hands, David sat, listening to his heart race. *Lord,* he prayed silently. *Please help Kathleen. I've hurt her so deeply.* Another face came back into his mind. *And Sarah, let me see her again, and take care of her, wherever she is.*

David didn't know whether he should report for work Monday morning. Mr. Harvey had always praised his hard work, but Kathleen came first in her father's mind. The man couldn't stand to see his daughter denied anything.

I'll have to clean out my desk if I'm fired, David told himself as he pushed open the oak door leading to Harvey and Merrit Investment Services. Typically early, David wasn't surprised to see the three other desks in the main office empty. Hearing footsteps, he turned to see Mr. Harvey standing in front of his office door.

"Young man, we need to have a talk!" Kathleen's father boomed, his corpulent frame filling the width of the doorway. "Come in here now!"

Following the man who'd been his employer for six years, David felt like he was being led to the gallows. When they'd sat down—his boss in the huge armchair behind his desk and David on a small chair in front—Mr. Harvey surprised him by smiling broadly.

"So, you're having second thoughts, my baby girl tells me."

"You don't know how badly—" David began.

"Just wait," said Mr. Harvey, still smiling as he held a hand up in front of him. "I want to tell you that I understand."

"You do?"

"Of course. It's natural for a young man to get cold feet." The office resounded with his deep laugh. "Don't tell Mrs. Harvey, but there was a time when I wondered what I was doing, giving up the carefree life of a bachelor."

Here I go again, thought David. "Sir, I'm not going to change my mind. I'm sorry that so many wedding plans were made, but I cannot go through with it."

The man's smile fell as his heavy-lidded eyes became cold. "One of the things I've admired about you is your stability. I take it, then, that you're serious, and you've thought of the consequences?"

Squaring his shoulders, David nodded. "If you mean my

job, sir, I don't expect to keep it after this."

Leaning back in his chair, Mr. Harvey drummed his fleshy fingers on the top of his desk as he stared at the young man. "I tell you what," he finally said. "I think you need a change of scenery."

"I beg your pardon?" said David, not quite believing his ears.

The smile came back to the man's face. "Kathleen's a high-spirited girl, and I've noticed she's a little bossy with you. It would do both of you some good to get away from each other."

"Away?"

"I need someone back in England for six months, maybe a little longer. I wanted to send you, but with the wedding—"

"You mean, I still have my job?"

Mr. Harvey laughed. "Of course, son. I'd be crazy to let someone like you go. Oh, I admit, I was all set to fire you, but that's no way to run a business. And what's more," he added with a wink, "I'm betting a certain young lady will be in your thoughts while you're away."

"Mr. Harvey, I want to be honest with you. This won't make me change my mind about the marriage."

"Never say never," said Mr. Harvey with a wink.

ten

"My dear, you're becoming quite skillful at this game." Mrs. Bowman tapped her finger on the side of the chess board. "You may beat me one day, if you keep making moves like that."

Sarah's face broke into a grin. "Was that a good move?"

"Well, no. I'll have your rook. But you get better every day, so don't be discouraged."

Sighing, Sarah studied her chessmen. Mrs. Bowman had insisted she learn the game, and Sarah was surprised that she enjoyed the challenge of playing. Hesitating briefly, she reached out and moved an ivory pawn forward, only to have the woman capture it with her knight.

"Take your time, now," said Mrs. Bowman. "You don't want to make another wrong move." The woman's complexion had developed more color since Sarah's arrival, almost a month before. After two weeks of switching trays with the girl, Mrs. Bowman had realized that she wasn't being poisoned. As her appetite improved, so did her disposition, and her headaches were disappearing.

Mrs. Bowman's son had also noticed the change, and the week before, Sarah had found a large box on her bed containing a beautiful mauve linen dress. When Sarah had discovered that the dress was from Jonathan, she'd felt uneasy. She didn't like accepting such a gift from a man.

However, when she'd approached her employer about the dress, he'd rolled his eyes. "Of course you can accept it! I'm just thanking you for taking such good care of Mother."

Looking down at Sarah with a smile, he'd added, "You've made such a difference around here."

"I can't tell you how much fun it is to have someone to play chess with again. Most of the women I know aren't interested." Mrs. Bowman's voice broke into Sarah's musings. "My late husband and I played often, and sometimes I beat him. I always wondered if he let me win."

"And you haven't played until I came here?"

"Oh, sometimes I talked Jonathan into a game, but he hasn't got the patience for it."

"What about the other servants?" asked Sarah. She noticed Violet was dusting the bookshelves that covered the west wall in the library.

"Don't refer to yourself as a 'servant,' dear," said Mrs. Bowman. "I like to think of you as my companion. But as to the Negroes, play chess, you said?" Her face turned solemn. "That would be cruel. Too much mental exertion. It taxes their brains and could give them fits."

Mrs. Bowman stood up. "I need to be excused for a minute. You should plan your next move."

Sarah wondered if Violet had heard what Mrs. Bowman said. She looked over at the girl, who seemed to have her mind on other things as she wiped each book with a cloth. *Mrs. Bowman is so good to me*, Sarah thought. *But I wish she wouldn't speak about the slaves that way, especially in front of them.*

Frowning at her chessmen, Sarah tried to anticipate Mrs. Bowman's possible countermoves.

"Move your knight over to take this pawn. It'll put her king in check," came a voice from beside her.

Sarah turned to find Violet studying the chess board, one hand on her slender hip and the other rubbing her chin.

"Violet? You know how to play chess?"

"Yes, missy. Been knowing since I was a little girl."

Sarah winced. "Violet, you said you'd stop calling me that. It embarrasses me!"

Hanging her head slightly, the slave asked, "Are you mad?"

Reaching out to squeeze Violet's hand, Sarah smiled. "Not if you tell me how you learned to play chess!"

"Back at the Riveroaks house — before I was sold here." Violet returned Sarah's smile. "One of Master Lucas's children taught me how."

"You've played it a lot?"

"Hundreds of times!" The sound of Mrs. Bowman's footsteps in the hall sent Violet back over to the bookcase. Picking up her dusting cloth from the shelf, she turned back to Sarah and whispered, "And I ain't had a fit in my life, ever."

Mrs. Bowman liked to retire soon after supper, and once she fell asleep, Sarah had a couple of hours to herself. Usually she sat on the back porch in a white wicker rocking chair, wondering at the goings-on in the slave cabins just north of the cornfield. Mrs. Bowman had told her that it wasn't proper for her to be near the quarters. Sarah could pick out individual families around the closest cabins only by their mannerisms and vague shapes, for their faces were blurred by the distance.

"Spinning wool?"

She turned at the sound of Jonathan Bowman's voice. "I'm sorry, did you speak to me?"

"I said your name, but you were apparently lost in thought."

"I was wondering about the people who live down there."

"Wondering?"

"Yes. How they live, about their families. They seem to care for each other a great deal."

"Callie—over there—she cares for her brood, too," said Jonathan, pointing to a calico cat stretched out against the woodbin, her stubby kittens scrambling over each other as they nuzzled against their mother for nourishment.

Sarah's eyes were grave as she looked into his. "Surely you don't think they're the same."

Jonathan shrugged his shoulders. He held his hand out to her. "Let's go for a walk."

"A walk? Where?"

"Wouldn't you like to see the cabins up close?"

Forty whitewashed cabins lined both sides of the lane. *Like beads on a necklace,* thought Sarah. About fifty feet apart, they had shingle roofs and brick chimneys. Behind each house was a vegetable garden. Most of the slaves were visiting in the yards or hoeing dirt clods in the gardens. "Hello, Massa Bowman" was the greeting from nearly every slave, and a small group of children followed from a bashful distance.

"Would you like to see the inside of one?" asked Jonathan, pointing to a house near the end of the row.

"Yes, but do you think they'd mind?"

"There's no one living there," he said casually. Walking to the front step, he lifted the leather cord from its wooden peg and pulled the door open. "Well, are you coming?" he asked, turning to look back at her.

The cabin smelled of emptiness and musky wood. It contained a good-sized front room with a fireplace, two tiny bedrooms, and a loft for the children. Sarah was at the bottom of the ladder leading into the loft, straining her neck to see as much of the children's area as possible, when she felt a hand on her arm. "You'd best not climb up there," said Jonathan. "The ladder looks in need of repair."

"Thank you," she said. "But I wasn't going to—"

Her sentence was cut off by Jonathan's mouth on hers. He pulled her close with his other arm. Sarah couldn't breathe.

She slid her hands against his chest and pushed him away with all her might.

"Mr. Bowman!" she said, wiping his kiss from her mouth with the back of her hand. "Why did you do that!"

Hurt washed across his face. Then, angry, his eyes narrowed. "It was just a kiss. Don't tell me you didn't expect it."

"I didn't!" she said, a cold chill racking her body. "I thought you were being kind."

He moved closer, a half-smile playing at his lips. "I thought that was very kind. Perhaps you'd change your mind in a little while."

Like a terrified deer, Sarah bolted past him through the front door. Dark-skinned children scattered as she ran blindly past the cabins. Their parents broke off conversations, gazing after her with knowing expressions. Nettie, a field hand, tightened her grip on the willow broom she'd been using to sweep her steps. *At least the white woman can run away,* she thought.

Jonathan strode toward the stables, his mouth set in a grim line. He could hear the familiar low neigh of his horse, Luther.

"Masta?" Isaac, the stableman stuck a dark head out from a stall. "I was just checkin' on this here colt 'fore turning in."

With a short nod, Jonathan opened the door to the tack room and reached for the closest bridle.

"You going riding this late, Masta?" asked Isaac, scurrying over to get Jonathan's saddle. Heaving it up into his arms, he pulled open the door to Luther's stall and stood behind his master, who was pulling the bridle over the horse's ears. "Gone to be real dark soon. You gone break a leg if you ride in the woods."

"Then I'll stay on the road," said Jonathan. "Here, hand me that saddle."

He rode the animal hard and fast down the river road. He

could no longer see the Ashley River by the light of the stars, but he could smell the water in the chilly night air.

Stupid of me! he berated himself. He should have been more patient. He'd planned to give Sarah a few more gifts like the dress, but the realization that his mother would be leaving for Charleston in less than two weeks had clouded his judgment.

The day he'd gone to Mary's for that handkerchief and seen Sarah standing in the door, her hair wild about her shoulders, he'd decided to enjoy getting to know her better. That his mother had been nagging him about hiring a white girl had worked into his plans perfectly. Now, beguiled by Sarah's beauty and innocence, he was becoming obsessed.

Pulling the reins sharply to bring his horse to a stop, Jonathan grinned. *This can work to my advantage,* he thought, turning the horse around and heading back for home.

"Miss Sarah?"

Sarah raised her head from her pillow. She didn't know what time it was or how long she'd been in her room. Recognizing the voice of Lucy, one of the house servants, Sarah said, "Come in."

Closing the door gently behind her, Lucy walked to the bed, the glow from her candle showing a face full of compassion. "You all right, missy?"

Sarah nodded, rubbing her eyes. "I'm going to be, Lucy." *As soon as I leave here and never come back,* she thought.

"Masta wants to see you in the library."

Sarah sat up in bed. "What!"

"He say to tell you that I'm supposed to come and stay in there with you."

Sarah was about to refuse when it occurred to her that this could be an opportunity to tell Jonathan Bowman that she was leaving for Charleston in the morning.

Sarah looked up at Lucy's face. "Do you think this is a trick?" She didn't know how much Lucy knew about what had happened earlier, but she knew from personal experience how much servants knew about what went on in households. Probably all one hundred eighty slaves had seen or heard about her running to the house in tears.

"No, Miss Sarah," she answered. "Don't look like one to me." Then she whispered something so low, that Sarah had to strain to hear it. "But be careful!"

"You may leave the door open, if you wish," said Jonathan, standing behind an oak armchair. He motioned to the sofa. "And please have a seat, both of you."

Silently, the women took their places. Lucy, ill at ease, folded her brown hands and stared at them, trying to blend into the room like the furniture. Sarah waited, watching Jonathan from the corner of her eye as he crossed to the front of his chair and sat down.

Leaning forward and resting his elbows on his knees, Jonathan studied his entwined fingers, choosing his words carefully. He looked up at Sarah.

"I apologize if you were sleeping, but I couldn't let the night pass without telling you how sorry I am for what I tried to do."

Though he looked sincere, Sarah had no pity for him. "I've no father, I can't read, and I've been a servant all my life," she said evenly. "Because of that, people have looked at me as lowborn since I was a little girl."

"But I don't—"

"Yes, sir, you do," she interrupted. "You think you can buy me a pretty dress and say pleasant things to me and then have your way with me because I'm too ignorant to know any better."

His face clouding, Jonathan opened his mouth as if to speak, but Sarah jumped in once more. "I don't have much, but the one thing I know is that I'm a lady. A lady, like my mother was. And you won't take that away from me, sir!"

Jonathan's blue eyes narrowed under their dark brows, and his face reddened. Then, as if willed back onto his face, his repentant look returned.

"I've been so wrong," he said.

Both Sarah and Lucy looked up with a start, though Lucy quickly lowered her head again.

Watch how you say this, Jonathan thought. *You may still have a chance.*

"You see, I've never had to chase women. Being unmarried and having this big home—well, women sometimes throw themselves at me." He lowered his eyes, as if ashamed by his admission.

"But then I saw you at the Carltons' house, and you were so beautiful and noble. I knew you'd be good for Mother, and I was right. You've brought peace back to this house.

"And, yes, perhaps the dress could be mistaken as a bribe, but I bought it only with the intentions of giving a gift to someone very special to me."

He lowered his eyes. "That's what you've become: special. I kissed you because I lost my head. And I know I said some ugly things afterward, but I was hurt because you didn't feel the same way about me. I'm in love with you, Sarah."

Sarah closed her eyes. "I'm sorry, sir, but I don't feel the same about you." She did not see the look of surprise that came over his face.

"You don't?"

"No. I'm sorry." Opening her eyes, she added, "And I want to leave in the morning."

"Please, no!" said Jonathan, sitting up in his chair. "It would kill Mother if you left!"

"I've thought of that, and I'm truly sorry, but it would be best."

"But you're going to Charleston soon, anyway. Planting season is in a month."

"I wish to go now," Sarah said firmly.

"All right, all right," he said. "Wait a minute." He settled back in his chair, deep in thought. "What if you and Mother left tomorrow?"

"You mean, stay with her in Charleston?"

"Yes," Jonathan said eagerly. "You wouldn't see me, and you'd have at least five months to decide whether to come back here or get another job."

"Will Violet be coming?" Sarah asked.

"She can, if you wish. Mother always takes one of the Negroes to keep house. Is that agreed, then?"

Sarah studied Jonathan's face. "Yes."

Jonathan held the door open for Sarah and Lucy to leave. When they'd gone, he walked over to the roll-top desk near the bookshelves. Grabbing a crystal whiskey decanter and a glass, he poured himself a drink.

Things hadn't worked out as he'd planned, but she wasn't gone for good—yet. He'd have to arrange a trip to Charleston once the crop was planted and be on his best behavior so Sarah would return in the fall. When she came back, he'd prove that he could be trusted.

Sloshing the amber liquid around in his glass, Jonathan frowned at the nerve of Sarah—a servant—thinking herself too good for him right after he'd claimed to love her. *It doesn't matter,* he thought, wondering why his hands trembled.

After Lucy had left her room, giving her hand a quick squeeze, Sarah felt her way to the bench at her dressing table. Lucy had offered to light the oil lamp, but Sarah wanted the darkness to cover her like a cloak.

He said he loves me, she thought, propping her elbows on the table and wondering why she felt nothing in return. *No man's ever told me that before.* Then she realized that one man had spoken of his love many times—if only in her dreams.

eleven

It's so good to be back home, Sarah thought, wrapping her wool shawl against the morning chill. Not even the fishermen were out on the wharf so early. Low fog shrouded the water, and in the distance, the sun's first rays turned the eastern sky pale blue.

The intense quiet sent a shiver through her. *Something's out there. I can feel it. Whatever is there, it—or he—wants me to find him. Could it be David?* Lost in thought, Sarah held out an upturned palm as if pleading for whatever was out there to give her something she could touch and understand.

Cold dampness on her cheek made Sarah realize she was crying. An unexplainable longing haunted her. Could it be God? Was He trying to talk to her? Where could she find Him?

Suddenly, Sarah knew where to look.

"I want you to teach me how to read."

Violet drew her head back as if slapped and set down the lamp globe she'd been cleaning. "What?"

Crossing the parlor to the eighteenth-century cherry bookcase, Sarah grabbed a book. "Words," she said, holding it out in front of her. "I need to read them."

"But missy—I mean Sarah—I can't do that."

"Are you going to tell me that you can't read?"

Violet sighed unhappily, hanging her head. "I can read. How did you know?"

Breaking into a grin, Sarah grabbed her by the shoulders. "One evening last week as I joined you on the porch, you suddenly blew out your candle. Later, I found a book under the cushion of the chair where you'd been sitting."

Violet's eyes widened. "You must be the one who put it back in the bookcase!" When Sarah nodded, Violet said, "I've wondered all week how it got there."

"So you'll teach me?" asked Sarah.

Fear covered Violet's face like a veil. "It's against the law for me to know how to read!"

"Against the law? Then how did you learn?"

"When I was a little girl, I was put with Master Lucas's crippled daughter, Becky. I helped her up if she fell down and held her hand when she climbed the stairs. Becky didn't want to go no place without me, and when she and her brothers learned their lessons from the tutor, I listened."

Violet's huge eyes filled with tears. "Becky died when she was about fifteen. That's when Master Lucas sold me. I guess I reminded him about his daughter."

"But you were a little girl. How could you know you weren't supposed to learn? Anyway, that's a silly law."

"The laws here got teeth, just like a bulldog, and I don't want to get bit," said Violet, her voice flat.

Undaunted, Sarah went on. "Mrs. Bowman's going to a meeting of the library auxiliary after breakfast. Then she's having lunch with some friends. We'll hurry through the chores, and we'll have—"

"But it ain't right," interrupted Violet.

"Is it against the law for me to learn to read?"

"I don't think so."

"And can you forget what you learned?"

"No, 'course not," Violet said, her face mirroring her confusion.

"Then how is it breaking the law for you to teach me to read?"

"Seems like it would be, that's all."

Taking a step closer, Sarah locked eyes with the younger girl. "Violet, I want to learn to read more than anything. Will you please, please teach me?"

Closing her eyes, Violet nodded.

"I was beginning to worry about you." Mrs. Bowman added a teaspoon of sugar to her cup of coffee. "You must have slipped out of here pretty early. Where did you go?"

"The wharf by the farmer's market," said Sarah, pulling out a chair as Willie Mae set a cup of coffee on the table in front of her.

Mrs. Bowman's eyebrows shot up. "The wharf? Promise me you won't go there alone again. Some of the people lurking around seaports are not to be trusted."

"I won't. I'm sorry if I worried you."

"That's a good girl. Now, I've told you about my plans for today?"

"Yes, ma'am."

"Judge Rarick may be coming for supper again, so I'd like you to remind Violet to set the table with the Wedgwood dishes."

"I will," said Sarah, knowing that she'd be doing it herself once her employer left. Mrs. Bowman's Charleston home—many times smaller than Magnolia Bend—required such little upkeep that one servant could keep the general portion of the housework done. Willie Mae, a white woman hired every spring, took care of the cooking and kitchen, while laundry was picked up on Mondays and returned on Wednesdays by Mrs. Turner.

Sarah's duties were to shop for groceries and supplies, help Mrs. Bowman dress, and be on hand for a chat or game of chess whenever Mrs. Bowman had a blank place on her calendar. Over Violet's protests, Sarah insisted on helping with the housecleaning, but she did it discreetly, so as not to upset her employer.

Sarah didn't understand why Mrs. Bowman had said, "It isn't good for Negroes to have white people performing servant jobs in front of them." For someone who could be so kind, her employer had horribly wrong beliefs about black people.

Sarah's reflections were interrupted—and reinforced—when Mrs. Bowman sighed and said, "I'd love to have Jonathan here with us. I do worry so about him being all alone."

Almost two hundred slaves, yet she feels he's alone, Sarah thought.

"And so Farmer Smith. . .plowed his corn fields. . .with. . . great care." Looking over the *Hartlet's Book of Elementary Prose* she'd bought in April, Sarah sought Violet's eyes. "Well?"

"That was good. You learn fast," said Violet, smiling.

"You're a good teacher. I think I'm ready now."

"Ready?"

"Someone I knew once gave me a notebook of things he'd written down. I've never been able to read it, but I'd like to try."

"Do you want me to help?"

Sarah gave Violet's hand a squeeze. "I haven't let anyone read it. Can you understand?"

Violet shrugged. "Course. We'd best be getting out of the kitchen anyway, before Miss Willie Mae gets up from her nap."

Hurrying quietly to her room, Sarah took the leather-bound notebook from her chest of drawers. Settling in a chair by her window so the June sun could light the pages, she opened the cover.

"Violet!" Sarah banged on Violet's cellar-room door.

The door opened immediately, and Violet, puzzlement showing on her face, let Sarah in.

"I can't read any of it!" Sarah cried, her cheeks splotched red. "Look!"

Taking the notebook that was thrust out at her, Violet opened it. Suddenly, she laughed.

"It's not funny!" exclaimed Sarah, bursting into a fresh torrent of tears.

"I'm sorry," Violet apologized. Turning the notebook so Sarah could see the pages, she explained, "This is script."

"Script? But that's not what you taught me."

"Not yet. It comes after you learn to print." Pointing to a letter, Violet said, "What letter does this look like?"

Sniffling, Sarah took the book from Violet. "Is it a *b*?"

Violet nodded, her face beaming. "Most of the script letters look like the printin' that you already know. It won't take long to—"

"I can't wait any longer!" said Sarah. "I want you to read it to me now."

The girls sat on Violet's quilt-covered bed and Violet turned to the first page of the notebook. "Gracious, Sarah. It's a book of Scripture!"

"Yes, that's what David said it was."

"David?"

"The friend who gave me the book."

Violet's dark eyes lit up. "I haven't seen a Bible since I came to Magnolia Bend. You don't know how I've prayed to be able to read Scripture again. Just listen, Sarah!" Clearing her voice, she read slowly and reverently:

> *My sheep hear my voice, and I know them, and they*
> *follow me: And I give unto them eternal life; and they*
> *shall never perish, neither shall any man pluck them out*
> *of my hand. My Father, which gave them me, is greater*
> *than all; and no man is able to pluck them out of my*
> *Father's hand.*

"My Father's hand," repeated Sarah, eyeing Violet's face thoughtfully. "You're a Christian, aren't you?" she asked. "Why didn't you tell me?"

"I wanted to, and sometimes I could feel the Lord telling me to talk to you about Him, 'specially when we'd study your reading together, but I was scared."

"Why?"

Violet wiped a tear from the corner of her eye. "Right before you came, Miz Dora used to be in a real bad way. She even accused us of poisoning her food! One day I was cleaning in her room while she was in bed, and she started crying."

Wiping her other eye, Violet continued. "I felt the Lord telling me to tell Miz Dora all about Him so she could learn to have joy—just like He's been telling me to talk to you. Only, when I tried to, she got mad at me and slapped my face. She said that somebody who don't have a soul shouldn't be so uppity as to preach to her mistress."

"Oh, Violet. I'm so sorry. I wish I'd been hit instead of you." After a long silence, Sarah asked, "You really can feel God telling you things?"

"Yes," said Violet. "I know that don't make a lot of sense, but—"

"No, it makes sense!" Sarah interrupted, grabbing Violet's shoulder. "Because I've felt something calling me, and I wondered if it could be God."

"Glory be!" exclaimed the slave girl. "That's how I felt before I got the new birth!"

Sarah shook her head. "Now you're not making sense."

A smile spread across Violet's face. "I'd best start at the beginning." She pursed her lips. "You see, God lives in a place called Heaven, where there's no sin—not even a little speck."

"I know about Heaven," said Sarah. "Mrs. Carlton told me about it. People go there when they die."

"Good!" said Violet. "But, the problem is we're all sinners, because we can't help but sin once in a while. We got that from the first man and woman, Adam and Eve."

"I've heard about them, too. They lived in a garden until they ate some fruit that God told them not to eat."

"So we've got that sin inside us, and remember what I said about Heaven?"

"Not a speck of sin," answered Sarah, her face solemn.

"Don't look so sad. That ain't all there is!" said Violet. "See, there was a man named Nicodemus who was real important back in Jesus' time. You know who Jesus is, don't you?"

"Yes. He was the Son of God."

"Not was," said Violet. "He still is. He was living in Heaven with God, the Father, but He came down to earth in a body like ours a long time ago. Anyway, Nicodemus felt that callin' that you and I felt. He couldn't sleep one night, so he went to where Jesus was staying."

Sarah's eyes filled with longing. "I wish we could do that."

"Wouldn't that be nice!" Violet said. "But we can still talk to Him."

"Prayer?"

"Prayer. And He can talk to us—if we listen—by making us feel things in our hearts that He's trying to tell us. We can read the things He said, too."

"Scripture," said Sarah.

"That's why I was so glad to see some," breathed Violet, hugging the notebook to her chest.

"But what about Nicodemus?" asked Sarah.

"Well, he was a mighty good man. He didn't kill nobody, went to church, and told the truth the best he was able. But he still wasn't satisfied."

Sarah's voice fell. "He knew there was something he needed, but he didn't know what it was?"

"And you know what that feels like," said Violet. "Do you know what Jesus told him? He told Nicodemus he had to be born again."

"But how?"

"That's just what the man told Jesus! And you know what he was thinking—that Jesus was telling him to be a little baby all over again." Violet rolled her eyes. "As if! You know what Jesus told him after that?"

Sarah shook her head.

"He said, 'That which is born of the flesh is flesh, and that which is born of the Spirit is spirit.' We're all born of the flesh, 'cause we're human beings. But the only way to get into Heaven is to be born of the Spirit. That means asking Jesus to save us, and when we do, He cleans the sin out of our hearts and sends the Spirit to live inside us." Violet leaned forward, studying Sarah's face. "Do you understand?"

"Some of it," she answered. "Mrs. Carlton had a little silver cross with Jesus on it. When I asked her about it, she said he died for us and came alive again three days later, but I didn't understand why."

Violet was thoughtful for a minute. "Do you remember just a little while ago when you said you wished Miz Dora had slapped you 'stead of me?"

"Yes."

"Well, Jesus did the same thing. He looked down at us from Heaven, and He seen that we was going to be punished for our sins. That made Him so sad that He told his Father, 'I wish it could be me to be punished instead of them.' That's why He came down and died on the cross. He took our sins on His own self, and shed His blood to pay for them."

"So how do you get born again?" asked Sarah.

"By asking God to let Jesus' sacrifice on that cross be for your sins, too, and trusting Him to do that."

"That's all?"

Violet grinned. "I know it sounds too easy, but He wanted it simple enough for an ignorant slave like me to understand."

Sarah grinned back. "Or an ignorant Brit like me. I want to think about all this." Reaching out and touching the leather cover of the notebook again, she asked, "Would you read some more to me?"

"For as long as you want me to," answered Violet.

Watching her friend's brown face filled with joy, Sarah remembered back to that terrible dinner party at the Nortons' *If God knows everything, He must know that I don't have a father,* she thought. *Does it matter to Him?*

Just then the sound of Violet's voice penetrated her thoughts. "A father of the fatherless. . .is God in his holy habitation."

Sarah had just walked through the front door with a basket of grocery parcels when she heard a familiar voice in the parlor. *Jonathan Bowman,* she thought, retreating.

"Sarah, is that you?"

Not able to pretend that she didn't hear Mrs. Bowman's voice, Sarah stepped into the den.

"Yes, ma'am," she said, ignoring the man who stood as she entered the room.

"Haven't you noticed Jonathan, here? I was just telling him how much Judge Rarick reminds me of him, don't you agree?"

Smiling through clenched teeth, Sarah said, "Judge Rarick is a gentleman."

"See?" said Mrs. Bowman, beaming up at her son. "Sarah sees the resemblance, too."

The corners of Jonathan's mouth curled up. "It's good to see you, Sarah. I've been here in town on business for a couple days, and I wanted to see Mother before going back."

"I don't know why you didn't stay with us," pouted Mrs. Bowman.

"This house is so small. I didn't want to make anybody uncomfortable."

"Well, goodbye, then," said Sarah. "I'd better put these groceries away."

"Wait." Jonathan held a hand up. "May we talk on the porch for a few minutes?"

Startled, Sarah looked questioningly at Mrs. Bowman.

"Jonathan told me you might be taking another position and not returning to Magnolia Bend with me in October. I don't think I could go back there without you," Mrs. Bowman said. "I told him to talk you right out of that foolish notion! If it's more salary you need—"

"I'll handle it, Mother." To Sarah, Jonathan said, "Would you please talk with me now?"

The two walked out to the porch, and Jonathan leaned his tall frame against the rail. "I don't think you're concerned about salary," he said, "but I'll be happy to raise it if you'll stay with Mother."

"The salary I receive already is more than generous," said Sarah, shielding her eyes against the bright August sun. "I must confess that I haven't looked for another job yet. I've been so happy here."

"Really?" His eyebrows lifted.

"Yes, sir. Violet has been teaching me about God."

Jonathan laughed. "I hope Mother hasn't heard her teaching you religion." Turning his back to the sun, he asked, "You think you'll be coming back, then?"

"I don't know," said Sarah. "I'm wondering if you. . . ."

"If I plan to act like I did last time?"

Sarah lowered her eyes. "Yes."

"I'll tell you what," said Jonathan. "You tell me how to act around you, and I'll do it. I promise."

"You promise?"

"I just said I did."

"I want you to leave me alone," said Sarah. "If I go back, you mustn't buy me any gifts or touch me."

"And you'll come back if I do those things?"

She sighed. "I want to think about it. May I have a week to decide?"

"Yes," he said. "Tell Mother your answer. And Sarah?"

"Yes, sir?"

"I'll be a perfect gentleman—just like Judge Rarick."

Pushing open the wrought-iron gate in front of the stuccoed house, Jonathan heard tapping overhead. Gazing down from a second-story window, Trudy was waving and smiling.

Has she been in that window all morning? wondered Jonathan, remembering how he'd waved goodbye at her from the street earlier. He'd evaded his mother's questions about where he was staying, knowing how appalled she would be if she discovered her son was staying with the notorious Widow Dalton.

Letting the gate swing behind him, Jonathan stopped. Squinting, he judged the distance the sun was from the horizon. *I could make it back to Magnolia Bend before dark if I started right now,* he thought.

The face behind the upstairs window looked confused. *What did I ever see in her?* Jonathan wondered. Her bawdy laugh irritated him, along with her insistence that she be with him every waking moment. It was a wonder she hadn't followed him to his mother's! *What would Mother have thought—or Sarah?* he mused, reminding himself that a servant's opinion didn't matter.

Touching the brim of his hat in farewell, Jonathan turned on his heel and went back through the gate to where Luther was tethered to a hitching post.

It's no use. I can't sleep! thought Sarah, punching her pillow. *If I don't decide soon, Mrs. Bowman might hire somebody to take my place.* The thought of being separated from Violet was too terrible to consider, but Sarah didn't want to constantly keep her guard up around Jonathan Bowman. And what if his sincerity had been an act? Sarah was determined that what had happened to her mother was not going to happen to her.

Slipping out from under her sheet, Sarah walked to the window and pressed her forehead to the glass. The moon was a sliver over the darkened houses lining East Bay Street. *I'm the only person awake in Charleston,* she thought.

If only she could talk to someone. She couldn't discuss her struggle with Violet, who'd told her that she'd run away if

Sarah didn't come back to Magnolia Bend. She didn't want Violet doing something that would endanger her life!

Suddenly, David's face came to mind. *I've got his office address in the notebook,* she thought. Hadn't he told her to come to him if she needed help? She remembered that day in Washington Park when she had seen him with the well-dressed lady. Perhaps he was married to her.

What difference does it make! Straightening, Sarah crossed her arms. *I'll just ask for advice as a friend.*

"Five more months!" exclaimed Kathleen Harvey, white spots rising on her flushed cheeks. "You told me David would be gone for only six months. It's already been four!"

Sighing, Mr. Harvey held out his beefy hands helplessly. "This assignment he's working on—I'll need him over there a little longer."

"But you said—"

"I know, I know. But he's doing a good job investigating opportunities, and he needs to go to Liverpool to close out an agreement. Good business can't be rushed."

Kathleen leaned forward, her clenched fists on top of her father's desk. "You'll let your own daughter suffer so you can make more money, is that it?"

Mr. Harvey slammed down his palm on a stack of detail papers, sending the top sheet flying. "Listen to me, young lady," he growled. "Making money is what I do well, which is a good thing because you and your mother spend it as fast as I make it. Now go count your dresses or something, and let me get back to work!"

Kathleen hurried from the private office, glancing back to see her father concentrating on his work as if she'd never visited. *I'll be an old maid, and what does he care?* She strode past clerks with their heads bowed over their ledgers as if they hadn't heard her father yell at her. She would love to slap them all for pretending to work while, inside, they were laughing at her! Throwing the front door open with all her weight, she nearly ran over a young lady.

"Why don't you watch where you're lurking!" stormed Kathleen, finally able to vent her wrath on someone.

"I'm sorry," said the girl. "I didn't expect the door to open so quickly." Her face brightened. "Perhaps you can tell me. Does David Adams still work here?"

Kathleen's mouth dropped open. *So, this is why David broke our engagement!* She lifted her chin haughtily as she studied the intruder. The waiting girl could be called pretty, though she lacked sophistication.

"David is overseas on business now," Kathleen said icily. "When he returns, we'll be getting married. He'll be too busy to entertain visitors."

"Oh!" said the girl, her face turning crimson. "When you see him, please tell him that Sarah Brown came by."

"I'll do that," said Kathleen as she turned on her heel to leave.

Mrs. Bowman looked up from the book in her lap when Sarah walked into the parlor.

"If you still want me, I'll go back to Magnolia Bend with you," said Sarah.

twelve

Never having seen Magnolia Bend in autumn, Sarah was unprepared for the burst of warm colors. "Is there any time that it isn't lovely here?" she asked Mrs. Bowman, who was seated opposite her in the carriage.

"I used to wonder that myself, but as I get older, I find it more and more difficult to leave Charleston," said the older woman, sighing. "I guess I'll always be a city girl at heart."

"Perhaps a certain judge has turned your head." Jonathan winked at his mother beside him.

"Oh, watch how you talk!" said Mrs. Bowman, gently slapping his hand and turning to address Violet. "And what did you think of Charleston?"

Violet's eyes shot open in surprise. "It was nice, Missus."

"Well, I'm certainly bringing you back next year. The house looked so nice. You practically did the work of two people!"

Had not Mrs. Bowman and Jonathan been seated across from them, Sarah would have burst into laughter. As it was, she averted her face and pretended to watch squirrels playing on a nearby limb. She knew that if she looked at Violet, they'd both have trouble keeping straight faces.

Later that evening, the girls unpacked Sarah's trunk. "How do you feel about being back?" Sarah asked.

"Maybe things'll be better around here—at least for the house servants. You sure have caused a change in the missus."

Sarah shook the folds out of her sea-green poplin dress. "I don't know what I did, except maybe have a good appetite."

"What?" Violet tilted her head to look at her.

"I'll tell you one day."

When the last dress and nightgown were put away, Sarah reached into the almost-empty trunk for her leather notebook. "I'll keep this in the top drawer of my chest. Whenever you want to read it, help yourself."

Violet flashed an easy smile. "You sure you don't need me to read it to you anymore?"

Shaking her head, Sarah smiled back. "I almost wish I hadn't learned to read script. Those days were special."

"It was the words that was special," said Violet. "You can't read the Lord's words without feeling a stirring in your soul." Her face grew serious. "Have you thought any more about asking for the new birth?"

"Many times, but I keep thinking I should wait until I feel worthier."

"Sarah, there most likely ain't anybody on this earth as good as you. You've helped me with my work, bought me those two dresses in Charleston, and you're just plain nice to everybody, colored or white.

"But," Violet continued, "compared to Jesus, none of us is worthy. We've all got some sin in our hearts. You've just got to repent—that means be truly sorry for your sins—and ask Jesus to cover them with the blood He shed on the cross. That way, when God looks at you, He don't see any unworthiness at all, just the purity of His own Son."

"All right," said Sarah. "I want to do that now."

"Glory be!" exclaimed Violet. "Do you want me to leave?"

"No, please stay. Do you think I could pray standing at the window? I'd feel closer to God if I was looking out at that sunset."

"I don't see why not."

Both girls stood at the window, feeling the nippy October air against their faces. "Should I pray out loud?" asked Sarah.

"Why don't you just be still for a minute and let God speak to your heart. Then you'll know how to do it."

Resting her hand on the windowsill, Sarah watched the orange rays of sunlight turn the clouds into hues as varied as the oak leaves in the lane. "Oh, Lord," she finally breathed. "I don't see why You would want me as Your child, but it says in David's notebook that You want to be my Father. Please forgive my sins and save me now."

When Violet didn't speak, Sarah turned to find her friend wiping tears from her eyes.

"Why don't I feel any different?"

"Feelings don't have nothing to do with it. It's what God promised in His Word that counts," said Violet. "But I think those feelings will come before too long. Wait and see."

Violet was right about the feelings, thought Sarah as she lay on her pillow later that night. *I feel like the part of me that was missing is here. At last I have a Father.*

"Have you ever ridden a horse?" asked Jonathan, holding out an apple for Sarah to feed to Lady.

"Oh. Hello, sir." Sarah took the fruit from his hand. The mare's nostrils quivered at the smell of the treat, and lowering her head over the stable door, she pulled the apple into her mouth, dripping juice on Sarah's hand.

"Don't wipe it on your shawl. I keep a handkerchief around for such emergencies," Jonathan said, pulling a square of linen from his shirt pocket. "Don't worry. It hasn't got yellow birds sewn on it."

Sarah laughed. "I'll clean your handkerchief and return it to you," she said.

"Well," repeated Jonathan. "Have you ever ridden a horse?"

"Never." She eyed Lady wistfully.

"Would you like to learn?"

"Now?"

"Why not?"

Her eager expression was quickly replaced by wariness. "No, thank you," she said, reaching up to rub the horse's muzzle one last time.

"Let me guess why," said Jonathan. "You don't want to be alone with me."

"Are you surprised?"

Kicking a piece of hay stubble with his foot, Jonathan sighed. "I suppose not. I guess you're never going to forgive me for my rudeness that day."

"Forgiveness is something I've learned a lot about lately," Sarah answered. "I can forgive you, but I would be foolish to put myself in the same situation again."

"What if we stayed on the river road and Isaac rode with us?" he asked, nodding toward the slave who was soaping a saddle a few feet away.

"Well," Sarah smiled at the dark-skinned young man. "Would you mind?"

Isaac gave a vigorous nod. "I like to ride horses."

Sarah's face fell as she turned back to Jonathan. "I haven't got a riding skirt."

"Mother used to ride all the time, and she's almost as slender as you. I'm sure she'll be glad to lend you one." Pointing to the house, Jonathan added, "Why don't you take care of that, and I'll help Isaac saddle up the horses." He turned to Isaac as Sarah left. "Bring me two bridles."

"Yassir," said the slave, coming around the sawhorse where the saddle hung. He'd only taken a step or two when he stopped, letting out a groan as he bent over slightly.

Sarah wheeled around at the sound of Isaac's cry. "What happened? Is he hurt?"

"It ain't nothing. I'll be fine in a—ouch!" he cried, trying to take another step. "I'm sorry, Massa," he said to Jonathan, his face a mixture of pain and disappointment. "My back give out this mornin' when I was chasing that one-eyed colt back in its stall. I don't see how I can get up on a horse."

"I'll get a couple men to help you to your cabin," Jonathan said. Turning to Sarah, he shrugged his shoulders. "Some other time?"

"Is he going to be all right?"

"Oh, don't you worry none, missy," said Isaac. "This ain't the first time it's happened. I just got to lay me down for a day or two."

Sarah was about to leave again, when she saw the look of concern for Isaac on Jonathan's face. *He cares about them after all,* she thought. Hesitating, she took a step forward. "We can still ride, if you want to."

"Are you sure?" Jonathan asked. "We wouldn't have anyone to go with us. I don't trust any of the Negroes but Isaac to ride my horses in the saddle."

Sarah nodded. "I'll go ask Mrs. Bowman about a skirt."

When she was gone, Jonathan turned to Isaac. "Come help me saddle these horses. Then stay out of sight for a couple days. Have Anson do your work."

Straightening up, Isaac brought some bridles from the tack room. "Massa," he said meekly as he held out a bridle. "I didn't like fooling the missy, there."

"Did I hear you say something?" said Jonathan, stopping to glower at the young slave.

Isaac looked down at his shoes. "No, sir."

"By this time of year, work changes on a rice plantation," Jonathan explained to Sarah as their horses sauntered down the dirt road. Over to their right and stretching out to the river were the rice fields, left in stubble from the harvest.

"The rice was shipped last week, and most of the food crops have been gathered. Before winter hits, we'll have the Negroes repair the dikes and mend cabins and fences. Repair broken tools, too. A little later, they'll be butchering the livestock."

They rode on in silence. Finally, Sarah spoke. "I don't understand how one person can own another."

Lifting an eyebrow, Jonathan looked over at her. "You're not an abolitionist, are you, Sarah?"

"I've been thinking about it a lot since I came to America, and yes, I believe I am."

"The Negroes here have it much better than the free ones in the cities up North," said Jonathan. "Their housing, food, medicine, and clothes are provided, and they get taken care of when they're old. How can you see anything wrong with that?"

Mindful that Jonathan was her employer, Sarah replied, "Sir, I worked for two different households in England. The first family didn't pay me anything, even though I worked hard helping my mother in the kitchen. The second family paid me a pittance, when that."

Taking a deep breath, she continued. "They provided all those things that you mentioned, but I was resentful when I got old enough to think about it. My life was not my own, but theirs— and to be had cheaply."

"But that was different. You could have quit."

Her eyes widened at his blindness. "Don't you see? That makes slavery much worse. Will you allow your workers to leave if they're not happy?"

"It doesn't work that way," he said crisply. "And besides, my people are happy."

There was another silence. *I've made her dislike me even more,* thought Jonathan. After all his planning to be on his best behavior and win her confidence, they were having an argument.

Surreptitiously, Jonathan drew back on the reins so that Luther would slow his pace. Sarah seemed not to notice that her horse was slightly ahead of his. Embarrassed by speaking so bluntly, she had turned her face toward the river.

Taking advantage of the opportunity, Jonathan studied Sarah unobserved. The steady November wind played with the hairs about her face, pulling out whispery tendrils from the thick braid which hung down her back. Her posture, surprisingly erect for one who'd been a servant all her life, showed off her tiny waist. Though he couldn't see them, he imagined her deep-set dark eyes, eyes which made him uncomfortable by their quiet assessment of him.

He'd seen more beautiful women, but none had captivated him like Sarah. *She's bewitched me,* he thought, a frown creasing his forehead. Why had he even brought her to Magnolia Bend? He'd been satisfied with life the way it was.

"We'd better turn around," Jonathan said, realizing how foolish it would be to "accidentally" get caught by the night. "It gets dark in a hurry this time of year," he added.

"Oh, yes," Sarah stammered, giving him an appreciative look. "I hadn't noticed."

When they'd turned the horses around and were headed back toward the plantation, Jonathan said, "I'm sorry if I was rude to you a little while ago."

"You weren't rude," Sarah replied. "I criticized the life you've had since you were born. Perhaps I had no right to speak. After all, slaves prepare my food and clean my clothes. But I will always think slavery is wrong."

"Then can we ever be friends?" he asked, his nerves growing taut when she hesitated.

"Yes, if you like." Sarah leaned forward to pat Lady on her neck. "I appreciate your teaching me how to ride."

"Then you'll come riding with me again?"

"I'd enjoy that very much."

Three weeks later, Violet came into Sarah's room with a bucket of glowing embers for the fire. "You awake?" she asked.

Sitting up in bed, Sarah kept the quilts up around her shoulders against the chill. "Yes. Thank you for the fire. Do you have time to read some of the notebook with me?"

Violet shook her head. "Maybe after supper's cleared up." Miz Bowman wants me to get with Trudy in a little while and let her teach me how to sew. One of the girls that helps Trudy make clothes for the servants, her eyes are going bad. I'm glad, 'cause I like to make things with my hands, 'stead of just cleaning all the time, but I might not be able to visit with you as much."

Having laid the ember and kindling, Violet sat on the edge of the bed and faced Sarah. "I need to talk to you about something."

"All right." Sarah studied her friend's face. "It's something serious, isn't it?"

"That depends. You been out riding horses a lot with Master Bowman lately, and that's got me worried."

"But he hasn't tried—you know—since we came back here."

"That's good," said Violet. "How do you feel about him?"

"Do you mean is there a romance between us?"

Violet nodded, her eyes grave. "It ain't none of my business, but—"

"We're just friends," said Sarah hastily. "I like him, but I'm not in love with him."

"You're sure?"

"Very. Now, what's this all about?"

Violet's shoulders relaxed. "I was worried that you were falling in love with him. Some 'round here say he's got an evil heart."

"Really? Why do they say that?"

"The field hands don't hardly talk to us house servants. They say we're uppity, and maybe some of us are when we shouldn't be. So we don't hear a lot of the talk that comes from the quarters. But I did hear that Master Bowman got in some trouble with one of the woman field hands a while back."

Violet put a couple logs over the blazing kindling in the fireplace. "I don't want to see you get hurt," she said, her back to Sarah. "I don't think a Christian should marry someone like Master Bowman."

"Marry!" Sarah laughed. "Violet, you were afraid I'd marry him?"

Turning, Violet's face was a picture of hurt. "Yes, I was afraid it might come to that."

"I'm sorry!" said Sarah, slipping out from under the covers to rush over and hug her friend. "I wasn't laughing at you! The idea of me wanting to marry Jonathan was so—"

"You called him Jonathan just then."

"Well, yes. He asked me to. But we're just friends. Besides, I talked to him yesterday about trusting Jesus, and he said he'd think about it."

"He did?" It was Violet's turn to look surprised. "Well, I guess if ole Saul can be changed, then there's hope for Master Bowman! Just. . .I hope it's 'cause he's really interested, and not just to get on your good side." Suddenly, she looked down at Sarah's feet. "Better get you some slippers on before you catch some kinda sickness!"

thirteen

"I want to spend a couple weeks in town," said Mrs. Bowman from the other side of the chess table. "The weather always turns nasty after the beginning of the year, so this is the last time I can go until spring. I'd like to do some Christmas shopping, too."

She's missing Judge Rarick already, thought Sarah as she moved a pawn diagonally. The quiet, gray-haired man had been by the house for Thanksgiving dinner. His bushy eyebrows looked comically out of place over a neat mustache, but Mrs. Bowman thought him the most handsome man in Charleston.

The transformation in Mrs. Bowman's appearance since she had met the judge that spring was remarkable. She fussed with her hair and dressed with great care. *Perhaps they'll get married,* thought Sarah, *and she can always live in Charleston, where her heart is.* Increasingly, Mrs. Bowman complained about the inconveniences of living in the country.

"I want you to come with me," she was saying. "We won't be taking any servants, as some good friends have invited me to stay with them."

Glenda Wallis and Murial Hinton were widowed sisters quartered in a brownstone on Barkley Street. Why Mrs. Bowman had wanted Sarah to accompany her remained a mystery to the girl. When Mrs. Bowman wasn't shopping and gossiping with the sisters, she was being entertained by Judge Rarick. Fixing Mrs. Bowman's hair and helping her dress were

Sarah's only responsibilities.

During her free time, Sarah explored the city. At a bookstore on Canton Street, she bought Violet a black Bible wrapped in brown paper. On the shopkeeper's recommendation, she purchased herself a copy of *The Pilgrim's Progress.* She had that book wrapped as well, for she still had to do her reading in secret. What would happen if anyone learned that Violet had taught her to read, Sarah didn't know, but she didn't want to risk her friend's life.

As she walked back from the bookstore, Sarah thought of the slave who'd been hanged for having an abolitionist pamphlet. Jonathan knew better! Would he send a young woman to the gallows as well? Why not? Any system that would force human beings to work in the stagnant water of the rice fields—without a share in the profits—would easily sacrifice the life of a slave who dared to take some control of her life.

Am I helping such a system by working for the Bowmans? Telling herself that the Bowmans would continue to own slaves whether or not she was in their employ wasn't working anymore. From reading the Scriptures in her well-worn notebook, Sarah had concluded that Christians had to take stands against evil, even if they stood alone or the effort appeared to be futile.

I should resign my position right now, she thought. Mrs. Bowman was much kinder to the servants, now that she realized they hadn't been plotting against her. *But what about Violet? I told her that I'd stay.*

That's when the idea hit her. She would buy Violet from the Bowmans! At first the thought was so repulsive that Sarah felt nauseated. But on further consideration, she realized it was the only way. *I'll pay for her, then set her free!*

"Free!"

The curious stare of the woman sweeping the sidewalk in front of the lace shop made Sarah realize that she'd spoken aloud. Giving the woman a wink, she hugged her packages and continued walking, resisting the urge to skip.

As she continued planning, Sarah realized she didn't know how much a slave would cost. Would the seventy-five dollars saved from her wages be enough? She bit her lip. Mrs. Bowman didn't run Magnolia Bend, so she probably had no idea.

I'll have to ask Jonathan when we get back, Sarah thought. *Please, Father,* she silently prayed. *Show me a way to help Violet gain her freedom.*

The clamor of wheels and hoofbeats brought Jonathan to his feet. Tossing his book back into the chair, he crossed the room and walked out the front door to the porch.

He paid no heed to the biting December chill that greeted him. Squinting, he struggled to glimpse down the oak-lined avenue. *They've come back early,* he thought. Had his mother tired of shopping—or of the judge? Had Sarah missed Magnolia Bend? It seemed like so much longer than a week since she'd gone.

Suddenly the farm wagon came through the shadows, and Jonathan could make out Jason's brown face and a couple wooden crates. Jonathan slammed his open palm against the top of the railing. Bolting down the stairs, he waved the wagon to a stop.

"Who sent you to town?" he demanded, glowering at the slave.

"Mista Gatewood sent me to see if these here tools he ordered last month was in."

"I'm supposed to know about supply trips. Why wasn't I told?"

Jason's face was a mixture of confusion and fear. "Mista Gatewood, he done already told you, Masta. This mornin' before I left, at the back door. Remember he asked if you be needin' anything else?"

One of the horses hitched to the wagon let out a snort, nodding his great head as if laughing at him. Narrowing his eyes, Jonathan studied the slave's face for any signs of mirth. Being embarrassed in front of a servant was a new experience for him, and he didn't like it. "Go on," he ordered.

"Wait a minute, Masta. I got some letters here, too," said Jason. "You wants me to bring them inside?"

"No. Give them here."

The wagon had only gone a few feet when Jonathan called out, "Jason!"

"Yassir?"

"Tell Isaac to have Luther fed and saddled first thing in the morning," he said, grinning at the envelope clasped in his hand.

David stood at the fore deck of the *Great Western,* watching the hull slice through the whitecaps. He'd be home in time for Christmas. Smiling to himself, he thought of the Christmas gifts he'd purchased in Europe for his parents and sister. He hoped he'd be allowed to take at least a week off from his job, to visit them in Jasper. *If I still have a job, after Mr. Harvey realizes I haven't changed my mind about marrying Kathleen.*

Sarah was well into the third chapter of *The Pilgrim's Progress* when a tapping sounded from her door. Closing the book, she pushed it under her pillow.

"Come in," she said, standing up and brushing the wrinkles from her blue calico dress.

"Miss Brown, you have a visitor," said Charlotte, a round-faced maid with rosy cheeks.

"Me?" There'd been visitors every day since Mrs. Bowman and she had arrived in Charleston, but none for her. Pausing at one of the dressers crammed into the room, Sarah glanced into the mirror. *Should I hurry and pin up my hair?* she wondered, knowing that it would take at least fifteen minutes. Deciding that it would be rude to keep her guest waiting that long, she picked up a boar-bristle brush and ran it through her thick chestnut hair. Then she ran down to the parlor.

"Mr., I mean, Jonathan."

Sarah smiled and nodded at Charlotte's offer to bring tea, then turned back to the man who was standing in front of an overstuffed sofa. "I'm sorry, but your mother and some of her friends are having breakfast at the Russell house."

"It's you I came to see," said Jonathan, taking his seat only after Sarah found a place in an opposite chair.

For the first time in weeks, her face became wary. "Why?"

"You received a letter yesterday. I thought it might be important." From inside his gray frock coat, he pulled out the envelope. "Would you like me to read it to you?"

It's David! The thought leaped into Sarah's mind as she started to reach out her hand. *Wait. You're not supposed to be able to read,* she reminded herself. Putting her hand back in her lap, she asked, "Would you mind?"

Jonathan tore open the envelope and unfolded some sheets of paper. Glancing through the letter, he frowned. "This is from my cousin, Elizabeth Mobley. She says that a letter arrived for you late this summer at her parents' old address, and she's just getting around to sending it on, from a Julie Martin."

"Miss Martin!" Sarah sat up in her chair, her face lit up. "Please, read it to me!"

"You have the most beautiful smile," said Jonathan, oblivious to the letter in his hand. He blinked as if startled by his words. "I'm sorry. I know you don't like me to talk like that."

Sarah was grateful for the arrival of the tea tray just then, making it unnecessary for her to respond. Though Jonathan had professed to love her months before, she hadn't believed he meant it. But during the fall, she'd noticed him staring at her while pretending not to and making excuses to be near her.

Could he really be in love with me? She hoped not, for he'd been so kind lately, and she didn't relish the idea of hurting him.

Turning to the enclosed letter, Jonathan began to read:

> *Dear Sarah,*
> *Forgive me for not writing sooner, but things have been quite busy around here. I want to thank you and your employer, Mr. Carlton, for giving me back my home.*

Sarah wondered what Miss Martin meant by that until she remembered a conversation she'd had with the Carltons. After she'd been with them for some months, she'd told them about how Miss Martin had suspected that her attorney had plotted with the Gertys to take away her home. Mr. Carlton had told Sarah that he'd write Miss Martin a letter, advising her to get another attorney and have the matter looked into. They'd not heard from Miss Martin since.

> *As Mr. Carlton suggested, I contacted a solicitor with a reputation for being honest, and he was sympathetic with my case. It took a full year of tracking down so-called creditors to discover that I hadn't been as deeply*

*in debt as my former attorney had stated and that it was
unnecessary to sell my house. From there, we informed
the constable.*

*During the investigation, Mrs. Gerty dismissed me
and I had to move into a boarding house, but it was
worth it! Mr. Gerty and his attorney were brought to
trial in June and are both serving prison sentences for
fraud and theft. Mrs. Gerty, alas, was sent to the insane
asylum near Crawford, as she caused quite a row when
the eviction notices were given.*

Miss Martin's letter went on to say that Agnes and Frances
were doing well, having received substantial raises in their
salaries. Ginny and her husband had come back to work. After
more words of gratitude to Mr. Carlton and Sarah, the letter
ended.

Jonathan grinned with amusement. "This Miss Martin
thinks you're quite a heroine! How does it feel to have
someone so deeply in your debt?"

"I owe her more than she could possibly owe me," said
Sarah, earnestly. "If it hadn't been for her, I'd still be working
for Mrs. Gerty back in Bristol."

"Oh yes, the one in the insane asylum. A rather interesting
letter. You'll have to tell me about these people."

Smiling, Sarah repoured his tea. "It's so good to hear that
they're doing well. I left them less than two years ago, yet my
life is so different now."

"Does that mean you're happy?"

"Oh, yes!" Sarah said. "God has been so good to me."

Leaning forward, Jonathan's expression was hopeful.
"Have I done anything to help bring about this happiness?"

"Of course. If you hadn't hired me, I wouldn't have met

Violet." Immediately, Sarah realized she had not given the answer he had expected.

"You and your mother have been kind to me, too. I shall never forget you."

Jonathan frowned slightly. "You sound as if you're going somewhere."

"No, not me, but I'd like to talk to you about something."

Jonathan sat with an air of expectancy.

"Would you, uh, consider," she stammered, "selling Violet to me?"

"What?"

"Violet. I have seventy-five dollars, and I want to—"

"I heard you the first time," Jonathan said, crossing his arms. "Has our little abolitionist decided she needs a slave after all?"

"Certainly not! I want to give Violet her freedom."

Leaning back in his seat, Jonathan laughed. "Such high ideals in a woman of—how many years? Only eighteen? So, you want to pay me so you can set Violet free."

"What's wrong with that?" Sarah said, lifting her chin so that she could look him in the eyes.

"Nothing, my dear. You have a tender heart, and I admire you for it. But Violet's not for sale."

"Why not?"

"Well, for one thing, you don't have three hundred dollars."

"That much?" she whispered, her face falling.

"A bargain price these days, I assure you."

Sarah wiped her eyes with the back of her hand. "It would take two years to save three hundred dollars."

"Seems like I'm always around when you need a handkerchief," Jonathan observed, reaching out to hand his over. "Actually, you'd only have to save two hundred twenty-five, since you said you have some already. But that's not the only obstacle. It's against South Carolina law to let slaves go free."

"But there are free black people in Charleston. I've seen them!"

"Yes," he agreed. "They were set free either long ago by people without any foresight or recently by provisions in their owners' wills."

"Their wills?"

"And you know what has to happen to carry out the provisions of a will. I'm not prepared to die so that Violet can pretend to be white."

Sarah's face reddened. "Have you any sympathy for these people?"

"Yes, I have. Some. But you can't change the way things have been for the past century."

Blowing her nose into Jonathan's handkerchief, Sarah shook her head. "I was so excited, and now it's going to take so long." Abruptly standing, she made a motion toward the door. "I'm sorry. I'm not feeling well. Can you let yourself out?"

"Wait," said Jonathan. "Please sit down. I know a way you can help her."

Taking her seat again, Sarah waited. Jonathan was struggling to find the right words.

"You could become her mistress another way."

The wary expression returned. "How?"

"By marrying me."

The blood in Sarah's body felt like it had turned to molasses, and her heart pounded.

"Don't you have anything to say?" asked Jonathan, testily. "You look like I told you to sleep in a graveyard!"

"I can't," Sarah finally said.

"Because you don't love me." He shrugged his shoulders. "Do you think me a moon-faced young simpleton? I know you don't love me. I'd prefer that you did, but I want you for my wife regardless."

Sarah looked down at her hands. "How would my marrying you help Violet? Even if I were her mistress, she'd still be a slave."

"Not if we let her go."

Jerking her head up, Sarah narrowed her eyes. "You just said that was against the law."

"We could take her with us on our wedding trip up North and forget to bring her back, with no one the wiser."

"You mean, just leave her?"

"With some money to help her get started." Grinning, Jonathan said, "Your seventy-five dollars should be enough, don't you think?"

"I don't know. It doesn't seem like a lot to live on."

"It seemed like a lot of money to you a few minutes ago. You were trying to buy a slave with it." He winked. "All right. I'll give her a hundred dollars too. I think that's pretty generous, considering I could sell her tomorrow for—"

"I'll do it," Sarah whispered, closing her eyes.

Jonathan tilted his head as if he hadn't heard her correctly. "Do what?"

"I'll marry you."

"Right now?"

Sarah's eyes shot open. "Now?"

"The sooner we get married, the sooner we can set Violet free." He studied her face. "You don't mind having a small wedding, do you? I find guests and all that tedious."

Shaking her head, Sarah murmured, "Where?"

"How about right here? I can find a minister who'd like to earn some extra money, and we can be married by this evening."

Sarah tried to think rationally. "Your mother. What would she think?"

"Of course," Jonathan said, slapping his forehead. "We need to make sure she's here. What will she think? She'll be delighted. She's been pestering me for years to give her some grandchildren. I suppose it'd be wise to wait until tomorrow morning. That way, you can pack for our honeymoon, and I can send for Violet. Would you like me to buy you a new dress for the wedding?"

It was all happening too fast. "No. I'll wear my green one."

"Be sure to wear your hair down around your shoulders," he said. "You said Mother is at the Russell house? I'll drop by and let her know our plans, so she can have the satisfaction of making a little fuss. She may insist on that new dress. Do you mind?"

"It doesn't matter," Sarah said flatly.

"Well, I'm off then." Jonathan rose to his feet. "Do you think you could spare a kiss for your fiancé?"

Obediently, Sarah stood, bracing herself. Taking a step closer, Jonathan put both hands on her shoulders, his blue eyes crinkling at the corners while a smile played about his lips. Bending slightly, he brushed her forehead with a kiss and was gone.

Sarah was trying on the new ivory silk dress when Mrs. Bowman called to her from outside the door.

"Sarah, dear, may we come in?"

"I'll get it," said Gretchen, the maid who'd been fastening the row of covered buttons on the back of the dress. Opening the door, she stepped aside for Mrs. Bowman and the sisters, Glenda and Murial.

"Don't you look lovely!" exclaimed Mrs. Bowman. "And

wait till you see what Priscilla is making for your hair—tiny satin roses with seed pearls."

Glenda pursed her lips. "The dress drags. We should have Priscilla take up an inch or so."

"Good idea," said Murial. Turning to the maid, she ordered, "Go tell Priscilla to bring some pins right away."

"I'll finish buttoning you up," said Mrs. Bowman, motioning for Sarah to turn around.

Murial nudged her sister. "We'll let you two talk. We have a lot to get ready by tomorrow morning."

"I'm afraid this is turning into quite a lavish affair, contrary to Jonathan's wishes." The last button fastened, Mrs. Bowman turned Sarah around by the shoulders. "Glenda and Murial are so excited that it's hard to keep things simple."

Sarah smiled. "I don't mind. How do you feel about . . . me?"

"To be blunt, a few years ago I would've thrown a fit. Marrying a servant is frowned upon by my friends. Does that offend you?"

"When you've been a servant all your life, you understand how things are," answered Sarah honestly. "I'm not offended."

Mrs. Bowman gave a relieved smile. "When you came to Magnolia Bend, I was ready to lose my mind. I can't believe I had you switch trays with me!"

"It wasn't without some fear at first," laughed Sarah.

Wiping the corner of her eye, the older woman continued. "Remember the nights when I was afraid to go to sleep, and you came in my room and held my hand? You didn't treat me like a crazy woman, and your calmness helped me get over my silly fears."

Impulsively, Sarah stepped forward and gave Mrs. Bowman a hug. "Who will play chess with you while we're gone?"

Mrs. Bowman winked. "You've become quite skillful, but

Judge Rarick is a master—or so he thinks. He's asked me to marry him several times, but I turned him down. I didn't want to leave my son for good until he had a wife."

"So, you'll reconsider the judge's proposal?" asked Sarah.

"Most definitely!"

Changing back into her blue calico dress and wool cloak, Sarah slipped down the winding staircase and walked quietly through the massive living room. She closed the front door gently behind her, then sat in the nearest rocking chair. *They can handle the rest of the wedding preparations without me,* she thought. *I'm going to wait right here until Violet comes.*

Resting her head against the high back of the rocker, she closed her eyes, listening to the sounds of carriages in the street. Something didn't feel right, now that she had time to herself.

"You told me you weren't going to marry Master Bowman!" Someone was urgently shaking her shoulder.

Blinking her eyes, Sarah looked up into the face of her friend. "Violet!" she said, jumping up to give her a hug. "I couldn't wait to see you. I've got wonderful news for you!"

Violet's eyes widened. "Wonderful news! Don't you remember what I told you about him?"

"Let's go for a walk before it gets too dark," said Sarah, glancing back at the front door. When they were out of earshot of the house, she explained. "I'm marrying him for your sake."

"My sake? Oh, Sarah. I thought you was sensible, but something's—"

"Just listen." Sarah held up a hand. "Jonathan said he'd set you free up North if I married him."

"Set me free?"

"Yes, free! We're going to take a schooner to Boston

tomorrow after the wedding, and you'll have enough money to take care of yourself until you find a job. A real job, Violet. You won't be somebody's slave!"

Violet didn't reply as they walked down the sidewalk lining Barkley Street. The shadows of the palmettos and magnolia trees were growing longer as the sun hugged the western horizon, bringing a noticeable drop in the temperature.

"Is your shawl warm enough?" Sarah finally asked, disappointed that her friend didn't seem excited.

Drawing the worn shawl tighter to her slim body, Violet looked at Sarah. "If it wasn't, would you give me your cloak?"

"Of course," she said, her fingers reaching up for the top button.

"And what would you wear to keep warm? My shawl?"

Confused, Sarah paused at the second button. "Yes, I suppose."

"Then I'd be warm and you'd be cold. But you'd be happy, 'cause you love me."

"What's wrong with that?" asked Sarah, coming to an abrupt halt on the sidewalk. "Why are you talking like this?"

Violet turned to face her friend. "You're giving me your cloak—your freedom—and taking my shawl—slavery. Did you think that I would be happy about that?"

"But I'm not going to be a slave!"

"Do you love Master Bowman?"

"Well, no," said Sarah. "But he promised to—"

"If you don't love him, then you're going to be his slave."

Sighing, Sarah reached for her friend's hand. "It won't be like that. He loves me, so he'll treat me well."

"And what about the things the field hands say about him?"

"Did you ever find out what he did?"

"No, but I don't trust him, and I don't want you to marry

him!" Violet's tone softened. "Sarah, have you prayed about this?"

"There hasn't been time," she answered, her face solemn. "I was so happy when he promised to set you free that I felt it was a good thing to do. Don't you want to have your freedom?"

The slave girl sighed. "It's what I've prayed for many times. But this way ain't right."

"I said I'd marry Jonathan, and it's too late to change things," said Sarah, her voice suddenly firm. "Let's enjoy our time together while we still have it." They'd walked a few more yards when she asked, "Do you still love me?"

"Yes, my sister," whispered Violet.

"I have something for you in my room. I was going to give it to you for Christmas, but—"

"You're givin' me the chance to be a free person. That's enough, don't you think?"

"It's a Bible," said Sarah. "I bought it yesterday, and you won't have to hide to read it, either."

"A Bible." Shaking her head in wonder, Violet put a hand over her heart. "I can't hardly take the joy that's runnin' through me right now."

Sarah's eyes became moist. "Would you sing for me one last time?"

As they walked hand in hand down the brick sidewalk, Violet's clear, perfectly pitched voice sang out through the evening shadows:

> *Gone to take that boat, 'cross the River Jordan*
> *For to see my Lord, for to see my Lord.*
> *His shining face will be there to meet me*
> *He'll say "well done," He'll say "well done."*

fourteen

"It's a good thing the weather held until we got back," said Jonathan, wincing at the clap of thunder that rattled the window-panes. "I hope the dikes hold up in the fields."

"Yes." Sarah's answer was a distracted murmur. Leaving the window, Jonathan walked to the chair where she sat staring into the fire.

"What's wrong with my girl?" he asked, kneeling to take her hands. "Are you thinking about Violet?"

Giving an unreadable look, she turned her eyes back to the fire. "I miss her."

"But this is what you wanted," he said gently.

Sarah nodded. "It is. But I didn't realize how much it would hurt. I haven't felt so lonely since my mother died."

Jonathan's heart sank. While he knew Sarah didn't love him, he'd figured that he could change that with time. They'd been married for almost a month, and though she was kind to him, he saw no flicker of love. *How long will it take,* he wondered, *before she loves me as much as I love her?*

Suddenly, he had an idea. "What if I took you to Boston to visit her?"

Sarah's eyes blazed with hope. "You would?"

"Yes, of course." Gratified by the success of his idea, he added, "We'll have to wait until fall, after the rice is harvested and shipped. Can you wait that long?"

"Oh, yes! I thought I'd never see Violet again," she said. "You're so good to me."

He pressed her hands to his lips, closing his eyes. "You've done more for me than I could ever do for you. I never realized how good it would feel to be this much in love.

"But Sarah, I want you to do something for me," he continued, his face serious. "If I can't go riding with you, don't go alone. The ground is frozen and slippery. If Lady slips and breaks a leg, you could be lost out in the cold. Take Isaac with you, but don't go alone."

"All right." Sarah ran her fingers through Jonathan's thick dark hair. "It's nice to have someone worry about me."

"It is?" His expression was hopeful. "You do care about me, don't you?"

She smiled. "I care about you."

The bell over the door tinkled a welcome as Violet walked into the shop. The sharp smell of fabric dyes greeted her nose. Stacked bolts of cloth covered shelves on three walls.

"May I help you?" The white lady coming toward her was young and had copper hair pinned loosely into a bun.

"I saw the sign in your window," said Violet, "and I'd like to apply for the job."

"I'm Louise Johnson. I own this shop. Have you worked as a seamstress before?"

Resisting the urge to look down at the floor, Violet kept her head level. "I learned to sew shirts at the plantation where I lived. They weren't much fancy, but my stitches were straight and even."

"What about dresses?"

"No ma'am, I ain't had a chance to sew on a dress." She glanced around the shop at the fashions hanging from smooth wooden posts. "I could do it, though."

The owner looked doubtful. "I need to hire someone with more experience with ladies' dress clothes. Perhaps you should try one of the tailor shops?"

"Ma'am," said Violet, taking a deep breath. "Why don't you let me work for one month? I have money to live on for a while, so I won't take pay during that time."

"Oh, I couldn't let you do that," said the lady.

Violet pressed on. "I can get a job at a shirt factory, but I want to make dresses. I love the feel of good cloth and the way colors are put together to make a dress pretty. If you'll give me a chance to prove it, I'll learn fast, and you won't be sorry you hired me."

The lady studied Violet's face. "Where are you from?"

"Charleston, ma'am."

"What is your name?"

"Violet Bowman."

"Well," said Louise Johnson, smiling, "I'll give you one month. You'll get a salary, but if I'm not pleased at the end of that time—"

"Yes, ma'am!" Violet's dark eyes shone. "Thank you!"

"But the way you see it, everyone is bad." Jonathan shook his head. "That's ridiculous, Sarah."

"I didn't say that. I said we're all sinners. Surely you'll admit that you've sinned at least once in your life."

"Well, of course I have—like everyone else," said Jonathan, moving his knight on the chessboard. "But that doesn't make me a sinner."

Sarah thought for a moment. "What if Lucy brought you some water and said that she let one of the dogs take a lap from the glass. Would you drink it?"

"Which dog, Luke?"

"I'm serious," Sarah said, crossing her arms.

"All right, let's see. No, I wouldn't drink the water."

"Why?"

He sighed. "Because it would be dirty."

"From just one little bit of dog saliva?"

"You're making some kind of point here. Would you care to fill me in?"

"Delighted to," she said with a smile. "If it takes just a drop of saliva to make a cup of water dirty, how many sins does it take to make someone a sinner?"

"Uh, fourteen?"

"One."

"And now you're going to tell me about Jesus dying for my sins again."

Pain washed across Sarah's face. "It's the most wonderful story I've ever heard, how someone so great could love us enough to do that. Don't you want to hear more about it?"

"Frankly, no," said Jonathan, reaching over the board to pat her on the arm. "If it makes you feel good to pray and do all that, I'm happy, really I am. But don't worry about me. I haven't been perfect, but I don't think I've done anything that would send me to hell."

Sarah sighed. Jonathan looked at her, wondering if he'd made her angry. After a long pause, he asked, "Did Mother tell you?"

"About Judge Rarick?"

Nodding, he added, "They plan to marry as soon as planting season starts, when she moves back to Charleston. Then she'll live there for good."

"He has a beautiful home, and she's happy in town. How do you feel about it?"

"I'm glad, of course," he said. "I just hope he doesn't expect me to call him Daddy."

"Daddy," she echoed, smiling.

Relieved that he'd brought a smile back to her face, he spoke again. "You'll need to leave with Mother in the spring. I'll come to Charleston as often as I can, but I won't want you around here then."

Her face solemn again, she gave a slight nod. "I'll pray that you don't get sick."

"Well, it can't hurt to have an angel pray for me," he said warmly. "But don't worry. I've never had so much as a cold."

"It's a small family gathering," explained Mr. Harvey.

David Adams watched his employer's eyes. They were confident, even smug. *He's used to getting what he wants,* David thought. *He fully believes he can get me to change my mind.*

"Sir," he said aloud. "I've made plans for tonight. But thank you for the invitation. Please give my best wishes to Mrs. Harvey and Kathleen."

"I don't remember saying anything about tonight," said Mr. Harvey. "The invitation is for tomorrow night."

"But you said," David exhaled audibly, his shoulders falling. "I'm afraid I can't come tomorrow night, either."

"Let me guess. You've got other plans?"

"No sir, I haven't. It's just not a good idea for me to see Kathleen."

"But you've seen her already. I watched you, young man, when she walked through the office yesterday. You did a good job of pretending to work, but you couldn't keep your eyes off her."

David ran a hand through his sandy hair. He hadn't noticed Kathleen, but he needed to say something that wouldn't cause Mr. Harvey to lose face. "She's a beautiful young woman," he replied truthfully.

"But you're not interested." His employer's face hardened. "So you plan to keep hiding from her, like a coward?"

David squared his shoulders. "I don't plan to hide from Kathleen. Because I don't accept your invita—"

"Then why haven't you been to church since you came back from England?" Mr. Harvey interrupted.

"I have been—every Sunday."

"We haven't seen you. What do you do? Hide up in the balcony with the coloreds?"

"No, sir." David cleared his throat. "I've found another church."

"What!" Mr. Harvey's eyes grew twice their size. "So that's why you've decided to reject my daughter! Don't tell me you've become a papist. What have you done, taken some strange vow of celibacy?"

His cheeks coloring, David rose from his chair. "I've simply joined a congregation of believers a friend told me about. Perhaps you'd like to visit us. We meet in a house on Allyson Street."

"That'll be the day!" Mr. Harvey snorted. Picking up a pen, he waved his hand at the door. "Proceed with your work, Mr. Adams."

"What did those men want, and why did they have those dogs?"

Jonathan turned away from the window. "What?"

"Those men—is anything wrong?"

Glancing back toward the window, Jonathan gave Sarah a distracted smile. "Albert Jordan lives about ten miles upriver. One of his slaves ran away, and Mr. Jordan wanted permission to look around."

"You think he might be hiding here?"

Jonathan shook his head, walking over to put his hands on his wife's shoulders. "They said he's been gone for a week. It'll be nigh impossible to track him in this snow."

A shiver ran through Sarah's body. Somewhere, a man was being chased by a dozen men with guns and dogs. "What will happen if they find him?" she asked faintly.

Jonathan's face was somber. "That's none of our business, and I don't want to talk about it."

Hesitating briefly, Sarah gave a nod, wondering why he wouldn't look her in the eyes. *He must realize I'm hoping the slave doesn't get caught.*

David was surprised to find Elizabeth Mobley standing in the open doorway instead of a maid. "Um, Mrs. Mobley?"

She absentmindedly smoothed the sleeve of her worsted mauve dress, elegantly cut, though a bit worn. "Yes?"

"Do you remember me? I'm David Adams. I looked at—"

"I remember you, all right." Her eyes narrowed. "You and your prissy little fiancée tried to cheat me out of a fair price for my house last year." A look of triumph came to her face. "Well, I sold it anyway, and got much more than you two were willing to pay."

"That's good," David replied, genuinely relieved. "I felt badly about the way we changed our minds."

"Well, now you can rest easy," she said sarcastically. "Good day to you."

"Wait." David put out a hand before she could close the door. "I was wondering if you could help me. I'm looking for a maid that worked for your parents, a Sarah Brown. I thought you may have heard something about her."

"Elizabeth!" A man's voice boomed through the doorway. "Shut the door. You're letting in the cold!"

"Please?" asked David quickly. "Anything?"

Glancing back over her shoulder, the woman sighed. "Was she the little girl from England?"

His face lit up. "Yes!"

"She got married a couple months ago," she said, just before the door clicked shut with finality.

"I'll only be out for a little while," said Sarah, kissing her husband on the forehead as he sat propped up by his pillow. "Isaac is going with me, so don't worry."

Jonathan's response was ambushed by a violet fit of sneezing. Wiping his reddened nose with a handkerchief, he said, "Be careful, and don't stay out too long."

"I'll stay with you if you'd rather."

"No," he said, waving a hand. "The horses could use the exercise. Anyway, I'm going back to sleep." He blew his nose again. "How long do these things last?"

"About a week," she said sympathetically.

"Wonderful."

"How about if I read to you this afternoon?" she asked. "I think you'd enjoy *The Pilgrim's Progress.*"

"That might be nice." His brow wrinkled as he rubbed the stubble on his chin. "You know, it amazes me how quickly you learned to read."

"I had a good teacher," she answered truthfully.

"But all I did was explain the alphabet, and two months later, you're reading books!"

She gave him a smile. "I'll be back before lunch."

"And you stirs a little sugar in the milk before you pour it on the snow," Isaac was saying as the horses padded their way through the morning woods on a blanket of snow. "The children likes it that way." He looked over his shoulder suddenly, as if embarrassed to have anyone else know what he was going to say. "I still likes it, too."

"My mother used to make that for me," Sarah said, smiling at the memory. "Sometimes with cream. I thought she made up the recipe herself, but I guess not."

Isaac's hearty chuckle pealed through the snow-numbed stillness. "Likely, children all over the world knows about it if they live where it snows. Maybe they all be thinkin' their mamas thought up the idea."

Her laugh was cut short when Isaac shot an arm out, trying to grab Lady's reins. "Let's turn around now, miss!"

Startled, Lady reared back on her hind legs, pitching Sarah onto the ground.

"Oh, what I done!" Isaac cried, jumping from Luther's back. He ran over to where Sarah was struggling to sit up in the snow. "Miss Sarah, is you all right?"

Dazed, she wiped her face on the sleeve of her coat. "I think I'm all right. Will you help me stand up?"

Taking her by the arms, the slave pulled her to her feet. "You can walk?"

Sarah nodded, trying a couple steps to be sure. "Why did you do that?"

"I'm sorry, missy," he said, his face stricken as he stepped over to take Lady by the reins. "Let's go back now."

"Why?" Brushing snow from her eyelashes, Sarah tried to see what had startled Isaac on the trail.

"You ain't going to want to see it."

"See what?"

"Never you mind," said Isaac, his voice respectful but firm. "I'll come back by myself after we gets you home."

Fear and the cold set Sarah's teeth chattering. As she put her left foot in the stirrup and swung into the saddle, she concentrated on staring at Lady's mane. She was just about to turn the horse around, when she glanced up.

"No!" she cried, her face draining of color. "Isaac, it's—"

"It's dead," said Isaac, flatly. "Let's go."

Everything inside of Sarah wanted to leave, but she couldn't tear her eyes away from what lay on the trail ahead of them.

"Miss Sarah?"

She shuddered. "Please go see if he's really dead."

"Masta gone be mad at me if I let you 'round that body." Isaac's eyes were wet. "That ain't something a lady needs to see."

"I'll tell him I made you. Please, Isaac."

She watched as reluctantly, Isaac climbed down from Luther's back. Lowering her eyes to Lady's mane again, she listened until his footsteps, muffled by the snow, ceased. "Is he?" she asked, her voice shaking."

"He done froze to death," sobbed Isaac.

Her eyes filled with tears. "Who is he?"

"I don't know. He's just a child."

"A child!"

Isaac was coming back, wiping his eyes with the back of his glove. "We can't help him, Missy Sarah. I'll come back with some of the others and get him." Catching Luther's reins, he looked over at her. "Let's go."

It had been almost an hour since Isaac, Mr. Gatewood, and two other men had gone back into the woods with horses and a wagon. "They must have gotten back by now," said Sarah to Jonathan, who was pacing the floor of the library. As soon as Sarah had run upstairs to tell Jonathan about the child, he'd dressed quickly and come downstairs.

"You look pale." Dorothy Bowman eyed her son. "Why don't you go back to bed. You're too sick to be up. We'll let you know—"

Her words were interrupted by a knock at the door. "Come in!" said Jonathan.

Betty, one of the downstairs maids, came through the door and held it open for Mr. Gatewood, the overseer. "Mr. Bowman," he began, his face solemn. "May we speak alone?"

Glancing at Sarah before starting for the door, Jonathan nodded "Come on. I'll get my coat and we'll go on the porch."

"You'll do no such thing!" exclaimed his mother. "Sarah and I will go upstairs so you can speak privately. You don't need to be out in this weather while you're sick!"

With a look of resignation, Jonathan shrugged his shoulders.

When he finally came up to their room, Jonathan looked numb. He walked over to the bed and lay down, not even removing his boots.

Rising from her chair by the fireplace, Sarah quickly stepped over to where her husband lay and put a hand on his forehead. His skin wasn't feverish. "Jonathan?"

He reached up with his right hand and took her hand, pressing it to his chest. "It was the runaway slave—Albert Jordan's."

Sarah gasped. "But that was a child we saw in the woods!"

"I didn't want to tell you that the runaway was a child. I was afraid it might upset you."

"A boy?"

"Yes."

"How old?"

"Ten."

"Ten," she repeated, sniffling. "Why did he come here?"

Jonathan looked at her. "I don't know."

Sarah was trying to coax Jonathan to eat some food from his lunch tray when the commotion began outside. "Listen!" she said, tilting her head. "Do you hear that?"

"What is it?"

"I don't know. At first I thought it was one of the dogs, but it sounds like a person."

Hitting the side of his head with the heel of his hand, Jonathan swallowed hard. "My ears feel stopped up. I can't hear anything."

"I'll go see," Sarah said, putting the dish of stewed peaches back on the tray.

"Wait," he called when she was near the door. "Maybe I should go too."

"I wish you'd stay in bed," she said, turning the knob. "I can ask Lucy what's going on." The sound grew louder as she pulled the door open.

"Who is that?" Sarah asked Mrs. Bowman, who was standing in her doorway.

"I don't know," she answered, her eyes wide. "Let's go down and see."

The sound—which could now be recognized as a woman shouting—grew still louder as they hurried down the stairs and through the living room. Several of the house servants were gathered at the large window near the front door.

"Who's out there?" asked Sarah, noticing that the noise had stopped.

They all turned to look at Sarah and Mrs. Bowman, their expressions uncertain. "Her name be Nettie," said a young girl. "She's havin' a bad spell."

The slaves moved aside from the window so that Sarah and Mrs. Bowman could see. Sarah could hear Jonathan's footsteps on the staircase as she stepped up to the glass.

Outside, a woman was struggling with Mr. Gatewood and Isaac, who were trying to prevent her from climbing the steps leading up to the front porch. The woman, though smaller than both men, was making some headway toward the steps. Suddenly, she started to scream again.

"You done killed him! Massa, you killed my baby!"

Sarah turned to look at Jonathan, who was right behind her, clad in his nightshirt and some britches he'd hurriedly pulled on.

"You killed him! You murderer!" screamed the woman outside.

In a flash, Jonathan was through the front door. "Take her away, Gatewood!" he barked.

Mr. Gatewood's face was red from effort as he struggled with the woman "We're trying, Mr. Bowman," he said breathlessly.

Sticking his head back through the doorway, Jonathan motioned to two male servants. "Ben! George! Help them!"

"I hates you, Massa! I hates you till I die!"

"Sarah, go back upstairs. You too, Mother," ordered Jonathan before disappearing through the doorway again.

About to obey, Sarah looked back through the window. The woman, overpowered by four men, had gone limp, her screams turning into deep, pitiful wails. The men half carried, half dragged her away.

Suddenly a huge black man came running up from the direction of the barns. He held out his arms as he got closer to the woman. "Nettie!" he cried, his voice thick with emotion. Nettie uttered one more cry of anguish, then fainted, her head dropping forward as the men held her upright.

"I'll take my wife, please," said the man.

Looking hesitantly at Jonathan, Mr. Gatewood ordered the slaves to release the woman. The large black man scooped her up into his muscular arms and with a glance at Jonathan, carried Nettie back to the slave cabins.

Sarah watched Jonathan step to the east end of the porch, his eyes glued to the black man and his wife. Cold air from the still-open front door gusted through the house past motionless figures.

The spell was cut by the sound of Jonathan's footsteps as he came back inside, closing the door behind him. Without a glance at the group assembled at the window he walked briskly through the room and up the stairs.

He sat slumped in a chair by one of the bedroom windows when Sarah clicked the door shut behind her. Though she didn't understand what was happening, she knew it was serious and that her husband had some guilt in the matter. *I have to know,* she thought, even as fear of what the answers might be made her blood run cold.

"Jonathan." He didn't move.

"Jonathan, what was she talking about?"

"Nothing," he barely whispered. "She's confused."

Anger stiffened her back. "Don't think me stupid. You tell me, or I'll go and find her."

Jonathan sat up, his blue eyes incredulous. "No, you won't. This has nothing to do with you!"

Suddenly, Sarah remembered Violet's warning about Jonathan having had some trouble with one of the woman field hands. The explanation came to Sarah in an instant, drying up any feelings of affection she'd had for her husband.

"The child was yours, wasn't he?" Sarah spoke in a flat, bloodless voice.

Jonathan's face registered guilt, but his expression quickly changed to one of misunderstood innocence. "My child?" His laugh was forced, hollow. "Do you hear what you're saying?"

Abruptly Sarah crossed to the peg where her cloak was hanging.

"Sarah, I forbid you to talk to that woman!" Jonathan said, rising to his feet.

"You do?" Her eyebrows raised. "Do you plan to lock me in this room for the rest of my life?" Holding her cloak in her arms Sarah stepped toward him. "Because that's what you'll have to do to stop me from finding out what happened!"

Jonathan's fists clenched at his sides. A great sob tore through him. "Sarah, don't hate me!" he cried, throwing himself into the chair.

Her jaw set, she took a step toward the door, then stopped. "Tell me the truth, then," she said softly over her shoulder. "The truth!"

"All right," he said, covering his face with his hands as he leaned forward. "Only, promise me that you won't leave me."

"I can't make that promise. Tell me now, Jonathan."

He nodded, sighing. "Please sit down."

When she'd sat in front of him, Jonathan looked at her, his face wretched. "The boy was mine. I sold him to Albert Jordan when he was seven, about three years ago."

Her face paled as her hand shot up to her heart. "Why?"

"Because he was beginning to look like me. It was embarrassing to see him running around with his blue eyes and light skin." After a pause, he said, "I wasn't proud of what happened, and the boy was a constant reminder."

"What did happen?" she asked icily.

"Oh, Sarah. Please don't look at me like that! I was only nineteen, and so drunk I couldn't see straight."

"Tell me."

"I came home late from a party at one of the plantations. Nettie—I didn't even know her name, then—was outside near the stables. I don't know why she was walking around at night. I would have left her alone if she'd ignored me and kept on walking, but she looked at me with fear on her face and took to running."

Taking a deep breath, Jonathan continued. "I was young, remember. I chased her on horseback, cutting her off every time she went in a different direction. It was funny to me, to see how afraid she was." He shook his head. "She didn't scream. If only she'd screamed, I'd have left her alone."

"So you raped her."

His eyes met hers. "I did right by her. When I found out that she was. . ., I bought back Jim, her husband, from the man I'd sold him to."

"You'd sold her husband?" Sarah demanded.

"I didn't know it at the time. Gatewood handles all those details for me. When he told me, though, I bought him back. I even paid more than I'd sold him for. They had other children, later."

Sarah looked past Jonathan. The raw ache she'd felt when her mother had left her at Mrs. Gerty's came back, bringing tears to her eyes.

"He wanted to see his mother," she said, her voice dull.

"What?"

"That's why he ran away. He missed his mother and died in the woods from cold before he could get to her."

Jonathan's hands began trembling. "How could I know he was going to run away?" he pleaded.

Studying his face, Sarah's eyes turned cold. "I don't know who you are."

"Don't say that!" he roared, starting to rise from his chair. "I'm your husband. I love you!"

Sarah shot to her feet, holding out a hand in front of her. "Don't come near me. I'm leaving."

"No!" He stepped toward her. "Sarah, let me make it right."

"Don't touch me!" she commanded as she backed up. "Are you going to make that little boy come alive again? You're an evil man, Jonathan."

He stopped in the middle of the room, his shoulders sagging. "If you leave me—" His voice broke. "I'll kill myself!"

She locked eyes with him. "All right."

"All right? You'll stay?" His face was incredulous, hopeful.

"No. Go ahead and kill yourself!"

fifteen

Isaac brought the trunk into her old bedroom in the Bowmans' summer home. "Set it right here, please," said Sarah, motioning toward a place on the floor near the chifforobe.

With a grunt, Isaac slid the trunk down from his shoulders. Straightening, he looked sympathetically at Sarah's red-rimmed eyes. "I'd best put the horses away 'fore it gets too dark," he said gently.

Sarah nodded. "That's a good idea. You shouldn't be traveling back this late."

"Miss Sarah?" Isaac took the brown felt hat from his head and clutched it in his hands. "I ain't goin' back in the morning."

"You're not?"

"No, ma'am. Masta Jonathan tole me to stay here so's I can look after you." Looking down at his hat, Isaac added, "I s'pose there's a room downstairs where I can stay?"

Sarah shrugged. "I don't need anyone to look after me, but I know you won't go back if he told you to stay." She walked toward the door. "I'll show you where the room is."

Isaac didn't move. "There's one more thing, missy," he said, still talking to his hat.

"Yes?" she said, pausing by the door.

"He tole me to give you this money," Isaac replied, reaching a hand into his back pocket, "so's you can—"

Her eyes flew open. "Money! He thinks I'm going to take his money!"

Isaac looked embarrassed. "Now, missy. How you gone to eat if you don't buy food?"

164

"I'll get a job and leave this house, too. His money's got blood on it, and I don't want it!"

"Yes'm," the young man said resignedly.

Later that night, Sarah tossed restlessly in her bed. She couldn't get the little boy out of her mind. What was it like to freeze to death? All alone in those cold, dark woods, did he cry for his mother?

If only she could sleep! She was exhausted, but her mind raced feverishly from one image to another. Why hadn't she listened to Violet? There could have been other ways to set her friend free. And why hadn't she prayed about it?

Wrapping a blanket around her shoulders, Sarah got up and tiptoed across the cold, oak-planked floor to the fireplace. She squinted at the mantel clock only inches away, but she couldn't make out the hands in the dark. Carefully, she picked it up and carried it to the window, drawing a curtain aside so the moon would illuminate the clock's face.

Four-thirty, she thought. *I may as well lay some fires.* She could have the house warm and be dressed by daylight. That would leave a full day to look for a position.

The house was used rarely in the winter, but Sarah knew a stack of wood was stored in a lean-to against the carriage house. Slipping on some woolen hose and leather slippers, she put her cloak over her nightgown and made her way to the kitchen door.

Shivering as the icy February wind stung her face, Sarah slowly advanced toward the lean-to, walking carefully on the slippery cobbled walk. The return trip was more difficult because the load of wood upset her balance.

Only a few feet from the kitchen door, she moved a little faster. She bent over slightly and raised her knee to support the load while she reached for the doorknob. The top log began to slide. She grabbed for it and lost her footing.

"Ouch!" she screamed as her arm hit the frozen ground.

"I think she's 'bout to wake up."

Sarah opened her eyes to find Isaac and a short, bald man at the side of her bed. "Who?"

"I'm Doctor Lemoine," said the man with a slight French accent. He nodded toward her arm. "Are you in much pain?"

Lifting her head from the pillow, Sarah looked down at her right arm. It was stretched out along her side and wound with a thick layer of white bandages.

"I've put splints on your arm so you can move it while the break heals, but you must be careful. Do you need some laudanum?"

"I don't think so, but thank you."

The doctor nodded, touching his mustache. "Nonetheless, I'll leave some here and check in on you next week."

Isaac returned to Sarah's room after seeing Doctor Lemoine to the front door. "Miss," he began, shaking his head. "You should'a let me tote that firewood."

"It's not your fault," said Sarah, managing a weak smile.

"Yes it is. I didn't think to bring in any wood last night." His eyes began to glisten. "I been bringin' you bad luck since yesterday."

He looked so miserable that her heart went out to him. "Isaac, it was good that we found the boy. He needed to be buried properly, not left out in the woods."

"But now you and Masta—"

"That's none of your doing. I found out what he's really like."

Isaac weighed his next words carefully. "I'm gone have to go out for a little while," he finally said. "There ain't hardly nothing in the kitchen, 'cept a little flour in the can and some molasses."

"You're not going to buy food with his money!" Sarah exclaimed, raising her head from the pillow.

"Now Miss Sarah, you got to think." Isaac held up both hands. "How we gone to eat if I don't get some food?"

Her head sank back into the pillow. Her rumbling stomach reminded her that she hadn't eaten since noon the day before.

"Go buy some food," she murmured listlessly, staring up at the ceiling.

The empty bottle crashed against the fireplace bricks, throwing glass slivers over the hearth and rug. "Who needs her anyway!" Jonathan bellowed, wiping the spittle from his mouth.

The knocking at his locked bedroom door had ceased hours ago. Maybe his mother had gone to town, as well. *Let them all leave!* he thought. *I'll burn the place down!*

His bleary eyes found the lavender nightgown Sarah had neglected to pack in her haste to get away from him. He jerked it from its peg on the wall. Stumbling toward the fireplace, he brought the gown to his face. Tears gathered in his eyes as he recognized the faint scent of rose water.

"I'll burn you, too!" Jonathan mumbled, pitching the gown into the blazing fire. Sparks flew as the gown fell against the orange logs.

"No!" Jonathan cried, lurching forward. Falling on his hands and knees, he reached into the flames. Oblivious to the pain, he grabbed the gown and pulled it onto the hearth, jumping up quickly to stomp out the fire with his boots.

He scooped up the scorched garment, then looked down in puzzlement at the red stain on its bodice. He turned over his left hand. A jagged shard from the broken whiskey bottle was imbedded in his palm. Wincing, Jonathan grabbed the glass with his left hand and pulled it out.

Maybe I'll bleed to death, he thought, cradling the gown in his arms. "No!" he murmured, "I didn't mean that!" Furiously, he pressed the bleeding wound against his chest. "Don't let me die without seeing her again!"

"I don't understand what all this is about," sniffed Dorothy Bowman. She leaned her head against the back of the Queen Anne chair. "I know it must have been a great shock to find the little boy in the woods, but haven't you been away long enough?"

Sarah's heart filled with compassion. "I'm sorry, but there's more to it than that," she said gently. "I'll never be able to go back to Magnolia Bend."

Mrs. Bowman's face fell. "You're not thinking about a divorce, are you?"

"I don't know. It hurts to think too much."

"If you could only see him, Sarah. He's barely left his. . .your room. He hasn't shaved or taken a bath in two weeks!" Mrs. Bowman covered her face with her hands. "I think he might be losing his mind!"

Slipping out of her chair, Sarah knelt in front of her mother-in-law and took her hand. "I know you love your son," she whispered, "but there's nothing I can do for him right now."

"I wish you wouldn't go slippin' out of the house in the mornin' without telling me," scolded Isaac. "That's how you got your arm broke, remember? I'm s'pose to be looking after you."

"I'm sorry. I won't do it again," said Sarah. "I only walked a couple of blocks, though, so you needn't have worried." She rubbed the back of her neck. "Will you loosen my sling a little for me?"

Isaac lowered the knot in the wide strip of muslin. "I've just took some biscuits out of the oven," he said. "I was worried they'd be cold before you got home."

"You're turning into quite a cook," Sarah answered, smiling. "Do I smell bacon too?"

"I believes you do!"

When they'd settled at the breakfast table, Sarah told Isaac about a sign she'd spotted over the door to a house on Allyson Street. "It said 'Worship Services every Sunday morning at ten o'clock,'" she said. "The house was a little larger than this one, so there can't be many people who attend. Would you still call it a church?"

"I reckon, missy. You plans to go there sometime?"

"This Sunday, perhaps. Why don't you come with me?"

Isaac looked uneasy. "I been wantin' to go to church, but maybe you should go by yourself the first time and make sure they don't mind me comin' too."

"If you like," Sarah said. "Isaac, are you a believer?"

"I'm 'shamed to tell you, but I am." He frowned, lowering his eyes.

"Why are you ashamed?"

" 'Cause I helped Masta play a mean trick on you a while back, and every time I look at you I remember how I lied."

Sarah thought. "Your back—it wasn't hurt, was it?"

"No, ma'am. It wasn't. And I knew about what Masta done to Nettie, but I let you go off alone with him."

There was an uneasy silence. "Well, he didn't try anything," Sarah finally said. "And I'm sure Jonathan made you do it."

"That don't make it right. You're s'pose to do right, even when you might get punished for it."

"Then I forgive you."

Slowly, Isaac raised his eyes. "Don't see how you can."

Sarah smiled. "We're supposed to forgive."

Isaac paused, as if weighing his words. "Does that mean you're gone to forgive Masta Jonathan?"

Sighing, Sarah answered, "I don't know."

The Allyson Street church met in the living room of Pastor John Varner's white clapboard house. Sunday morning, some members came early to gather chairs from all over the house into the living room. One morning, people had begun filtering through the front door as David Adams was setting up the last chairs.

"David, is John upstairs?" asked Mrs. Oliphant, a kindly middle-aged woman who stood at the door to take coats and hats from people as they arrived. "We have a visitor this morning."

"I think so," said David glancing over his shoulder. "I'll go—" He froze. The young woman standing at the door had her back to him as Mrs. Oliphant helped her remove her shawl, but the long chestnut hair flowing from under a straw hat looked familiar. The woman turned around.

"Sarah!" David said.

"You know each other?" asked Mrs. Oliphant, looking from his glowing face to her startled one.

David took the young woman's left hand. "We met a long time ago." To Sarah, he asked, "Do you remember me?"

"Why, yes," she stammered. "David from the ship."

"What happened to your arm?"

She smiled, sheepishly. "I slipped on some ice last month."

"I'm sorry," he said, his brow furrowed with concern.

"It's almost healed."

"Wonderful! Would you like to sit down?"

When about thirty people were seated about the room, the worship service began. Sarah listened as David's clear baritone joined with the other voices and sang hymns. She was not familiar with them—the songs Violet had sung for her were the only ones she knew about the Lord—but she thought them beautiful.

I can't believe I'm sitting here next to David, Sarah thought. Her happiness at seeing him was suddenly marred by feelings of guilt. *I'm married. Perhaps he is, too. I shouldn't be this close to him.*

After the singing, Pastor Varner, a bearded man of about fifty, stood at the front of the room. His text was the story of the prodigal son from the book of Luke. Sarah listened to the story about the son who wasted his father's money on sinful living. Tears came when the pastor told of how the father forgave his son and welcomed him back into the family.

Lord, Sarah silently prayed. *Are You telling me to forgive Jonathan? How can I? What he did was so awful!*

When the sermon ended, David introduced Sarah to Pastor Varner and his wife, as well as to some other church members. She smiled when they asked her to come back the next Sunday, knowing that she could not. But when David offered to walk her home, she agreed.

They'd taken only a few steps down the sidewalk, careful not to walk too close to each other, when David asked about her husband.

"I was married in December," Sarah said.

"Why didn't he come with you?"

"He's not a Christian," Sarah answered truthfully, not wanting David to know the unhappy details of their separation.

"I'll pray that he will be one day," said David. "And what about you?"

"The Lord used your book of Scripture and a good friend to draw me to Him."

"I'm glad." They turned the corner onto Oakdale Street. "Perhaps you could persuade your husband to come with you next week."

Sarah didn't know how to respond. "David," she began, "I was happy to see you this morning, but I won't be coming back to your church."

"Why?"

"It's best that I go somewhere else to worship. I'll find another place."

He stopped on the sidewalk, under the bleak shade of an overhanging birch tree. "Will you tell me the truth if I ask you something?"

"Yes."

"Is it because of me?"

She nodded slowly. "It is."

Reaching a hand toward her cheek, David drew back suddenly. "I've wondered about you for so long. Tell me, have you thought about me at all?"

"Many times," Sarah said, tears forming in her eyes.

"Then, why didn't you contact me before you decided to get married?"

"I went to your office, but you were in England." Sarah swallowed hard. "I met a lady who said she was engaged to marry you."

"Kathleen." Pain covered David's face. "That's been over for a long time."

"It has?"

He took a deep breath. "We weren't right for each other, and I couldn't get you out of my mind."

"You couldn't? But you never tried to find me."

"Like an idiot I waited too long. When I did, Mrs. Mobley told me you were married."

They resumed their walk in silence, oblivious to the horses, carriages, and wagons that passed by. Too soon, they were at the wrought-iron gate in front of the house. David unfastened the latch and held the gate open. "You know, you could come back to my church," he said impulsively. "We could sit apart and not speak to each other."

Tears ran down Sarah's cheeks as she closed her eyes. "I don't think I could bear it!" With that, she turned and made her way through the gate to the house.

David watched her disappear through the front door, his fists clutched at his side.

"Did you speak to her?" The question was out of Jonathan's mouth before his mother could get down from the carriage.

Dorothy Bowman's face was grave. "Yes."

"How is she?" he asked, reaching up to offer a hand to his mother.

"The splint is off." Dorothy stepped to the ground. "Her arm looks good, if a little pale, but she has a haunted look."

"Do you think it's because she misses me?" he asked, daring to hope.

Mrs. Bowman shook her head regretfully. "Let's go inside, son. I'm rather tired."

Arm in arm, they walked toward the front steps together. "I was able to persuade her to stay in the house," she said. "It took some doing, but she finally listened. I told her that it would embarrass me greatly if she took a job, especially as a servant."

"You gave her the money?" he asked as they entered the front door.

"I gave it to Isaac. She doesn't want to admit to herself that you're supporting her."

Mrs. Bowman took off her cape and gloves, hanging them on the hall tree. "She won't be coming to my wedding—not with you there." She sighed. "I wish one of you would tell me what happened to cause this unhappiness. I know it had something to do with the little boy who died, but, sad as that was, I don't understand how that could keep you apart for two months."

"I don't understand, either," he mumbled.

Jonathan was spending more time in bed, leaving control of the plantation to Preston Gatewood. It was unusual for Jonathan not to check the rice fields for the coming spring planting, but he felt uncomfortable around the field hands. Although they were respectful, he could see the accusation in their eyes, and when they lowered their voices to each other, he imagined they were talking about him.

He had started keeping himself clean, again, but only after becoming nauseated at his own stench. The simple acts of grooming and dressing himself required more effort each day, and his appetite was waning.

She said I was evil, he told himself repeatedly. *She doesn't understand. I never meant to hurt anybody.* He knew many planters who had relations with their Negro women. It wasn't talked about, but almost every plantation he'd visited had a handful of light-skinned children. Compared with most slave-owners, he'd been a model of restraint.

If I could only talk to her again, I could make her understand. Every time that thought came to Jonathan, he'd remember his mother's warning: "She said she'll leave Charleston for good if you try to see her."

"I'm beginnin' to worry," said Isaac as he walked inside the kitchen with a basket of groceries.

A long string of potato peeling plunked into the bucket at Sarah's feet. "About what?"

"I keeps on seein' that same white man on the sidewalk 'cross the street. He was out there just now, but when he seen me comin' he walked away."

Setting the paring knife down, Sarah lifted a hand to her throat. "Do you think Jonathan has someone watching me?"

Isaac looked worried. "That did come to my thoughts, but why would Masta do that?"

"I don't know. What did he look like?"

"Nice suit of clothes, but not real tall." He motioned toward his head. "And he's got that light-colored hair."

Sarah clutched the edge of the table with both hands, fighting the consuming urge to run outside. "I know who it is," she murmured.

"Ma'am?"

"He's someone I used to know."

"You pathetic dolt!" David said under his breath as he walked the four blocks to his office. "Spending your lunch hours hoping to get a glimpse of a married woman!" How had he let himself become so obsessed with someone he shouldn't be thinking about? He felt a pang in his heart. How long had it been since he'd prayed? What kind of Christian was he, really?

Slipping into a dark alley a few yards down from his office, David got down on his knees, ignoring the pebbles that pressed sharply against the cloth of his pants.

Father, forgive me for not keeping my heart in tune with Your will, he prayed silently. *I ask for the strength to stay away from Sarah's house. And please take care of her.*

sixteen

Sarah was taking the carriage back from St. Michael's Church when she caught a glimpse of a woman who looked like Mrs. Bowman. Just as she was about to ask Isaac to stop the horses, she got a better look at the woman's profile. The unfamiliar face turned and looked at her, as if wondering why she was being stared at.

She's probably left for her honeymoon by now, anyway, Sarah thought, sitting back in her seat. *I hope her marriage is happier than mine.* Four months was a long time for a married couple to be apart, and Sarah knew things couldn't stay as they were for much longer. Yet she hated the thought of going back to Jonathan.

It would have been easier had he been cruel to her. *He made me feel special, cherished,* she thought. *I could have been content—even happy—with the man I thought he was.*

Jonathan waved Lucy away when she approached him in the library with a tray. "Not hungry," he said, wiping his face with a handkerchief.

"Your mama tole us to make sure you eat your meals," she said timidly.

"What?"

"Leah done cooked fried chicken and dressing for you."

"Why do you care if I eat?" he growled. "You'd all be happier if I starved to death!"

When she made no response, he narrowed his eyes.

176

"Wouldn't you?"

"No sir."

"Well, everybody else would! How long are they going to hold this grudge?"

"Don't know, Masta," said Lucy, placing the tray on the coffee table. "You gone to eat now?"

With a shrug, he moved to a chair near the food. "Wait a minute," he said as Lucy turned to leave.

"Yes, Masta?"

"Why aren't you mad at me, too?"

"Ain't my place to judge you. Fact is, Masta Jonathan, I feels sorry for you." Fear flashed across her face. "I better go now," she said, lowering her eyes as she took a step back.

"No," he ordered. "Sit down."

Obediently, Lucy perched her slight body on the edge of a straight-backed chair, her eyes fastened on the hands she'd clasped at her knees.

"Oh, relax, Lucy! You look like I'm going to hit you!" he said through clenched teeth. "You've lived here since I was a boy. Have I ever mistreated you?"

She shook her head. "No, sir." After a pause, she added, "You ain't never mistreated the dogs and horses, either."

"And what's that supposed to mean?"

Lifting her chin, Lucy asked, "How many children do I have, Masta Jonathan?"

"I don't know—three or four," he said impatiently.

"Five children, all grown. I had six, but my youngest died eight years ago."

"I remember that, Lucy. He drowned while swimming in the river."

"Charles. We didn't get to bury him," she said, her tired

eyes watering. "But I carry this around with me all the time." She reached behind her head and untied a leather cord, pulling it out from under her dress. "This here has a button from his shirt inside," she said, holding up the cord so that a small cloth pouch dangled from it. "When I gets to missing him so much that I can't stand it, I takes out this button and holds it to my cheek."

Jonathan fidgeted in his chair. "You've carried that around your neck for eight years?"

"Sometimes I has to make another pouch, when this one gets worn. Don't know why, but it helps some." Tying the cord back around her neck, she looked at Jonathan again. "I'd give up the rest o' my life if I could have him with me for just a day, Masta. Just a day."

A big tear rolled down Lucy's cheek. "We colored folks loves our children, just as much as white people loves theirs. We ain't like the hen out in the coop. She forgets about her first batch of biddies when another hatchin' comes along."

When he didn't speak, she continued. "And the colored children—they loves their mammas and daddies. I was 'bout thirteen years old when I came here on a boat from New Orleans with some other slaves. I thought my heart would wear out from grieving for my folks."

"When my father died," Jonathan said softly, his eyes staring blankly at the wall, "I cried every night for weeks, where no one could hear me." He was quiet for a spell, lost in thought. Abruptly he sat up, startled that he'd spoken out loud. "Take the tray back, Lucy. I don't have an appetite in this heat."

She'd retreated to the door when Jonathan stopped her. "Wait."

"Yes, sir?"

"You said you felt sorry for me a while ago. Why?"

"Because you 'bout the loneliest man I ever seen."

Jonathan hugged his arms together under the sheets. How could it be so cold? He'd roasted from the July heat all day, yet suddenly he was too cold to get a quilt from the chest just a few yards away.

A picture of worn fingers caressing a pouch flashed across his mind. Just as quickly, another image took its place: a boy, shivering. What had Lucy said? "Colored children—they love their mammas and daddies."

The little boy had set out, all alone, because he missed his mother. Did he know who his father was? Did he wonder about his blue eyes and straight dark hair? Jonathan clutched the top of the sheet as a dreadful thought hit him. *I didn't know his name!*

"I believe I'd like to go fishin' in the mornin' — get us a big mess of perch to fry." The steady motion of Isaac's straw fan matched the thump of his rocking chair against the front porch floor.

"Perch would be nice," said Sarah. She pointed over the treetops. "The evening star is out rather early. See?"

Isaac's attention was on the horse-drawn wagon pulling to a stop in the street in front of the house. "Looks like we have company," he said, rising from his chair. "Why, it's Anson and Lucy from the house!"

Anson's face was grave as he jumped down from the wagon seat and came through the gate.

"What's wrong?" asked Sarah as she stood up.

"He's dreadful sick, ma'am. The doctor won't come out

to the river durin' plantin' season, so Mista Gatewood said to bring him to you. Mista Gatewood says he can't leave right now, 'cause too much work in the fields."

Hurrying down the walk with the two men, Sarah went to the wagon and peered over the side. On a mattress under several quilts was her husband. His cracked lips were open and his eyes closed. His face nearly matched the white pillowcase on which his head rested.

"Is he dead?" Sarah asked.

Lucy shook her head. "Not yet. Can you send Isaac for a doctor while we bring him in the house?"

An hour later, Dr. Lemoine frowned, putting his hands in his pockets. "Malaria. Why has he waited so long to get help?"

"Lucy, one of the servants, said he wouldn't let them," Sarah explained. "He told them he didn't deserve to live. The overseer finally made them bring Jonathan here."

"Well, I think he's better off here than in the hospital," said the doctor. "Give him a dose of this medicine every three hours, and I'll check on him every day. Don't give him so many covers. It runs his fever up."

"I didn't dream it. You came to see me," Jonathan murmured, watching Sarah through half-opened eyes.

Sarah brought an enamel basin to the side of the bed. "Do you know where you are?" she asked as she squeezed water from a cloth and put it on his forehead.

His eyes flitted to the windows. "Charleston."

"You don't remember coming here yesterday?"

"No." A weak smile came to his lips. "You're here with me, Sarah."

She reached under the quilt for his hand. "Are you thirsty?"

"Thirsty," he echoed, but he wouldn't let her leave him to get a glass of water. With her free hand, Sarah managed to dip a clean cloth into the water in the basin. She brought it to his lips, squeezing out a few drops.

"We've sent a message to your mother," she whispered. "I don't know when it'll reach her, but—"

"New York," Jonathan mumbled. "Wedding trip."

Her eyebrows shot up. "You remember?"

"My mind isn't completely gone," he said slowly, and dropped off to sleep.

An hour later Jonathan woke again. "Please give me another quilt," he asked through chattering teeth.

Sarah turned away from the curtain she'd just opened. "You're awake?"

"Cold."

"I'm sorry, Jonathan, but Doctor Lemoine said only one quilt." She crossed the room to sit on the side of the bed. "You want to get better, don't you?"

"I'm not going to get better."

"Of course you are!"

He gave his head an almost imperceptible shake. "Will you forgive me?"

"Forgive you?"

"For what I did." Tears welled up in his eyes. "You're right. I'm an evil man."

"I forgive you," Sarah said, taking his hand.

"Not enough. Can't undo it."

"Sometimes you can't." Sarah wiped her cheek. "But I still forgive you."

The corners of Jonathan's mouth turned up slightly. "You forgive me? I love you, Sarah."

"I. . .I love you too," she said truthfully.

He closed his eyes for a minute, but when she thought he'd dropped off to sleep, he opened them again.

"I'm going to die."

"Don't say that!" exclaimed Sarah. "You're going to get well."

"Sarah," he whispered, turning his face toward her. "I'm scared. I've been having dreams."

"Bad dreams?"

"I don't know what's going to happen to me after. . ."

Sarah's heart lurched. "Jonathan, ask Jesus to forgive you. I know He will," she said urgently.

New tears came into his eyes. "Can't."

"You can't ask?"

"Can't ask. You don't know some of the things I've done."

"Jonathan, He'll forgive you if you ask Him."

"Why would he?"

"Because He loves you."

"No."

"Yes!"

Lord, Sarah prayed silently. *Help him understand.*

"Jesus let people kill Him so people like us could be saved," she explained. "And He's in Heaven now waiting for you to ask Him to save you. Please, Jonathan!"

He was silent. Finally, he nodded slightly. "Show me how."

Sliding closer to him, Sarah laid her head gently on his shoulder. "Lord Jesus," she prayed between quiet sobs. "Please forgive Jonathan of his sins and cover them with Your precious blood so he'll appear spotless before our Father in Heaven. Save him, Lord."

She felt Jonathan's hand in hers tremble. Lifting her

head, Sarah moved closer to his lips so that she could hear him.

"Lord, I'm not worth it," he whispered. "But Sarah says You'll forgive me if I ask. Please, forgive me—and save my soul."

With her fingers, Sarah wiped the tears from Jonathan's cheeks and stroked his hair.

The next day, Doctor Lemoine drew Sarah aside. "Give him all the blankets he wants," he said gently.

"But you said—" Suddenly, Sarah understood. "Is there no hope?"

The doctor shook his head. "Perhaps if I'd seen him earlier. Just keep him comfortable."

"How do you feel?" asked Sarah, forcing lightness into her voice. She took the bowl of beef broth from Lucy and brought it to Jonathan's bedside.

"Clean," he rasped. "Feel clean." He managed a smile through trembling lips. "But still cold!"

"This warm soup will help." She turned to Lucy. "Please get more quilts."

Lucy gave a meaningful look before going over to the chest. "Plenty of warm quilts in here, Masta Jonathan," she said softly.

After he'd had most of the broth, Jonathan asked for Isaac. "Go tell Mr. Earl Powell. . .my attorney. . .on Beech Street."

"You wants him to come here, Masta?" said Isaac, his brown face a picture of sadness.

"Yes. Tell him, now."

When he'd left, Jonathan turned his head away from the broth that Sarah held near his mouth. "Don't want more.

Want to talk to you alone."

Sarah nodded to Lucy, who took the dinner tray and left. "Why do you want to see your attorney, Jonathan?" Sarah wondered if he'd guessed how close he was to dying.

"Never made a will," he whispered. "Want to make sure Magnolia Bend goes to you."

She couldn't speak for a moment. "Please, don't," she said. "I don't want to own any slaves."

"Want to free them."

"What?"

"Let them go. When the rice comes in, divide money up so they can go North."

"Jonathan, you believed in slavery," Sarah said, still in shock. "Why are you doing this?"

"Want to make things right." He coughed, then, with some effort, gave her one of his old grins. "Okay?"

"Yes," she said, her voice trembling.

"You can live in this house. Lease plantation to company from town. They'll use hired workers. Tell them, let the old Negroes stay if they want to."

Nodding, Sarah put her hand on his cheek. "Don't worry about me," she said softly.

One blue eye winked at her. "You don't worry about me, either. Not afraid anymore."

David had read about her husband's death in the *Chronicle* some six months earlier. In spite of the many times he'd wished Sarah hadn't gotten married, he felt for her pain.

He yearned to see her, but he recognized her need to mourn. So many times he'd been tempted to walk on her street and try to catch a glimpse of her.

With a sigh, David set the box of hymnals down. Church was about to begin. Their tiny congregation was growing, and there were plans to start work on a church building when weather got warmer. Most of the members were married. *What would it be like,* he wondered, *to have Sarah by my side every Sunday?*

"David?"

He wheeled around. She was standing in front of him, a smile lighting her beautiful face.

"I didn't think you'd come back," stammered David.

"Neither did I, at one time. Do you mind?"

"Not at all," David replied. "Will you sit with me? And may I walk you home?"

"Yes, I'd like that," she answered, and the two joined the other worshipers.

They didn't have another opportunity to speak privately until after the service was over.

"I had to leave my job," said David as they walked down the sidewalk, the January wind turning their noses and cheeks red. "But I found a better one right away. I work for someone you may know, a Matthew Wesley."

"Mr. Carlton's shipping company!"

He nodded. "I have to travel quite a bit up and down the coast, but I like seeing different cities."

She looked over at him. The same boyish grin that had charmed her two years earlier was on his face. *I hope I did the right thing,* she thought. *He must realize why I came to his church today.*

They reached an icy patch on the sidewalk, and David shyly offered Sarah his arm.

"You know," he explained. "Mr. Wesley said when he hired me that if I ever got married, I could take my wife on business trips."

"Your wife would probably enjoy traveling with you. Will you ever get to Boston?"

"At least twice a year. You like Boston?"

"Yes," she replied. "A good friend lives there."

"Boston, New York—all kinds of places. It'd be fun, wouldn't it?" He covered her hand and squeezed it. "I'm afraid I don't get to travel this time of year, though. Weather's too bad."

"Well, do you know how to play chess?" she asked.

"Yes. I like chess."

"Then, if you ever get married, your wife probably won't mind staying home with you in the winter."

A Letter To Our Readers

Dear Reader:

In order that we might better contribute to your reading enjoyment, we would appreciate your taking a few minutes to respond to the following questions and return to:

Karen Carroll, Editor
Heartsong Presents
P.O. Box 719
Uhrichsville, Ohio 44683

1. Did you enjoy reading *Shores of Promise*?
   ❑ Very much. I would like to see more books by this author!
   ❑ Moderately
   ❑ I would have enjoyed it more if

   _____

2. Where did you purchase this book?_____

   _____

3. What influenced your decision to purchase this book?
   ❑ Cover   ❑ Back cover copy
   ❑ Title   ❑ Friends
   ❑ Publicity   ❑ Other _____

4. Please rate the following elements from 1 (poor) to 10 (superior).
   ❑ Heroine ❑ Plot
   ❑ Hero ❑ Inspirational theme
   ❑ Setting ❑ Secondary characters

5. What settings would you like to see in Heartsong Presents Books?

   _____

   _____

6. What are some inspirational themes you would like to see treated in future books?

   _____

   _____

7. Would you be interested in reading other Heartsong Presents Books?
   ❑ Very interested
   ❑ Moderately interested
   ❑ Not interested

8. Please indicate your age range:
   ❑ Under 18 ❑ 25-34 ❑ 46-55
   ❑ 18-24 ❑ 35-45 ❑ Over 55

Name _____

Occupation _____

Address _____

City_____ State _____ Zip _____

HAVE YOU MISSED ANY OF THESE TITLES?

These additional titles in our Romance Reader series contain two complete romance novels for the price of one. You'll enjoy hours of great inspirational reading. Published at $7.95 each, these titles are available through Heartsong Presents for $3.97 each.

____ RR2 A MIGHTY FLAME &
       A CHANGE OF HEART by *Irene Brand*

____ RR3 LEXI'S NATURE &
       TORI'S MASQUERADE by *Eileen M. Berger*

____ RR5 SONG OF JOY &
       ECHOES OF LOVE by *Elaine Schulte*

____ RR7 FOR LOVE ALONE &
       LOVE'S SWEET PROMISE by *Susan Feldhake*

____ RR9 SUMMER'S WIND BLOWING &
       SPRING WATERS RUSHING by *Susannah Hayden*

____ RR10 SECOND SPRING &
       THE KISS GOODBYE by *Sally Laity*

Great New Inspirational Fiction
from HEARTS♥NG PRESENTS

Biblical Novel Collection #1
by Lee Webber
Two complete inspirational novels in one volume.

_____ BNC1 **CALL ME SARAH**—Can Sarah, like Queen Esther
be used by God . . . even as a slave in Herod's place?
     CAPERNAUM CENTURION—One Centurion's
life is irrevocably changed by his encounter with a
certain Nazarene.

Citrus County Mystery
Collection #1

by Mary Carpenter Reid
Two complete inspirational mystery and romance novels in one volume.

_____ CCM1 **TOPATOPA**—Can Alyson Kendricks make an historic
village come alive . . . without becoming history herself?
     DRESSED FOR DANGER—Roxanne Shelton's
fashion designs were the key to her success . . . but
did they unlock a closet of secrets?

*BOTH COLLECTIONS ARE AVAILABLE FOR $3.97 EACH THROUGH
HEARTSONG PRESENTS. ORIGINALLY PUBLISHED AT $7.95 EACH.*

Send to: Heartsong Presents Reader's Service
P.O. Box 719
Uhrichsville, Ohio 44683

Please send me the items checked above. I am enclosing
$_____(please add $1.00 to cover postage and handling).
Send check or money order, no cash or C.O.D.s, please.
To place a credit card order, call 1-800-847-8270.

NAME _____

ADDRESS _____

CITY / STATE_____ ZIP_____
BNC1/CCMC1

LOVE A GREAT LOVE STORY?

Introducing Heartsong Presents —
Your Inspirational Book Club

Heartsong Presents Christian romance reader's service will provide you with four never before published romance titles each month! In fact, your books will be mailed to you at the same time advance copies are sent to book reviewers. You'll preview each of these new and unabridged books before they are released to the general public.

These books are filled with the kind of stories you have been longing for—stories of courtship, chivalry, honor, and virtue. Strong characters and riveting plot lines will make you want to read on and on. Romance is not dead, and each of these romantic tales will remind you that Christian faith is still the vital ingredient in an intimate relationship filled with true love and honest devotion.

Sign up today to receive your first set. Send no money now. We'll bill you only $9.97 post-paid with your shipment. Then every month you'll automatically receive the latest four "hot off the press" titles for the same low post-paid price of $9.97. That's a savings of 50% off the $4.95 cover price. When you consider the exaggerated shipping charges of other book clubs, your savings are even greater!

THERE IS NO RISK—you may cancel at any time without obligation. And if you aren't completely satisfied with any selection, return it for an immediate refund.

TO JOIN, just complete the coupon below, mail it today, and get ready for hours of wholesome entertainment every month.

Now you can curl up, relax, and enjoy some great reading full of the warmhearted spirit of romance.